The Silver Foxes

Nancy Swing

*For Keri
With thanks for
all your help.
xo
Nancy*

PARK PLACE PUBLICATIONS
Pacific Grove, California

First trade paperback edition November 2019
Designed by Patricia Hamilton
Manufactured in the United States of America

Published by
Park Place Publications
Pacific Grove, California
www.parkplacepublications.com

ISBN: 978-1-943887-97-2
Printed in U.S.A.

Cover photo: Shutterstock

For Russell

Let me count the ways …

BOOKS BY NANCY SWING

Malice on the Mekong 2016

The Lewiston, West Virginia Trilogy
Child's Play 2017
Lazarus 2018
The Silver Foxes 2019

ACKNOWLEDGMENTS

First and foremost, a big thanks to Patricia Hamilton who published all four of my books. Last year, with *Lazarus*, what with an unexpected death in family and organizing part of our town's celebration of Indie Author Day, I had to rush to meet my submission deadline. Hard to believe, but I neglected to thank her. So here it is for all time: *Thanks, Patricia Hamilton!*

Warm thanks to fellow West Virginians who gave me "technical advice": Nancy Van Gilst Rice on playing bridge; Rick Wilson on mineral rights, modern methods of surveying and toning down how Fred swears; Bob Swiger for help with playing golf, developing property and especially for suggesting long ago that I not write three stand-alone books but a trilogy with continuing characters.

Terry Piotrkowski and Ben Sternberg joined Rick and husband Russell Sunshine as "beta readers" — those marvelous helpers who read an almost-there draft and offer feedback. The final draft reflects many of their valued comments.

All that having been said, any errors or shortcoming in this last book of the West Virginia trilogy are mine alone.

1

"BASTARD'S LYING."

Throughout the blond oak pews, faces turned and glowered. Lips pursed and hissed, "Shhhhhhhh."

Alice Dundee swiveled her arthritic shoulders toward the speaker, ready to reprimand his cursing.

But Trudy, on his other side, was faster. Alice's friend reached out a wrinkled hand to touch his wrist. "Language, Fred."

"Well, I don't give a good goddam. He's a bold-faced liar."

Alice inclined her shaggy gray head until her lips were an inch from Fred's hearing aid. "Perhaps he is, but this is not the time. We're here for Suzie."

Out of the corner of her eye, Alice glimpsed Charlie Coleman, another of Suzie's friends from the Evergreen Retirement Community, leaning forward. He set his mouth in a straight line and nodded once in emphatic agreement.

Alice sat back, smoothed her navy sweater-coat down her lap and focused on Rodney Cunningham. Lewiston's premier property developer was winding up his eulogy in the pulpit of the Lewiston Baptist Church. He was certainly dressed for the part, she reflected, white shirt gleaming against black suit and tie.

Rodney's fervor filled the air. "I always prayed Suzie and I would be reconciled, and Jesus answered my prayers." He paused to run a hand down the silver of his carefully groomed Van Dyke, as if he might be holding back strong emotions.

"Praise the Lord," said the lady in front of Fred.

"Hallelujah," said the one behind.

Fred opened his mouth to speak, but Alice put an admonishing finger on her lips. The cloying scent of flowers banked six feet high threatened to turn her stomach, so she forced her attention back to Rodney's oration.

"I knew the Lord was with me when I went into that hospital room. And sure enough, Suzie asked me to get down on my knees."

Fred snorted, and Alice squeezed his fingers so hard he winced.

West Virginia's early autumn sun slanted through a stained glass window, bouncing off Rodney's bald head like a halo. "We held hands, and we prayed together." Rodney raised his arms toward the light. "Friends, I felt God take her. He released Suzie from her suffering."

"Thank you, Lord, thank you," said a man across the aisle.

Rodney clasped both hands in front of his chest and bowed his head over the urn of Suzie's ashes. "My beloved wife died in the arms of Jesus."

Alice lifted her chin and looked at him through slitted eyes. The perfect picture of a man unable to go on. Probably just the effect he wanted.

Once the benediction had been pronounced, Suzie's friends strolled to the church hall under leaves just starting to hint at red and gold. They filed along the condolence line, saying all the right things to Rodney and his two daughters. Alice had been concerned about another outburst from Fred, but he managed to say something appropriate to Brenda and Penelope, ignore Rodney and move on.

The four friends continued to the catered buffet for some coffee and finger food. Then Alice piloted them over to a corner table and sat down with a sigh. The weakness in her left side left by a childhood bout with polio made it hard for her to stand for long.

"Suzie was such a kind, gentle soul," Trudy said. "So hard to believe she's gone."

"Never met anyone more generous," Charlie added. "Years ago, when the track team needed funds, she just wrote a check and asked me to keep it anonymous."

Fred raised his upper lip in a snarl of disapproval. "Too bad we can't say the same for Rodney. Only people he ever helped out were his own spoiled brats."

Trudy frowned. "Let's remember where we are, Fred. We just went to a funeral."

Alice scanned the hall with its plain white walls, dark carpeting and florescent ceiling lights. Lots of Evergreen folks had come. Not just the Director, but also part-time staff like Bethanne Swanson. Volunteers, too. Eden Jones representing the EverTeens. Greg Pendergast who always had a hand in everything. Most everyone was on the opposite side of the hall, clustered around the sweets. No one close enough to hear.

"So much of what Rodney said is troubling," Alice said. "Suzie wasn't that kind of get-down-on-your-knees Christian. Going to church mostly meant fellowship for her, being with like-minded people on Sunday morning. She was wary of using religion as a crutch."

Trudy stopped nibbling at her tea sandwich. "Well, yes, she did say that, but maybe she didn't really believe it, especially with death near. Could Rodney be right?"

Fred put both hands on the thighs of his perfectly creased trousers, elbows akimbo. "Goddam liar." The retired dentist looked ready to yank every tooth in Rodney's head.

"Suzie was fine when I saw her that morning," Alice said. "Talked about being discharged the next day, coming back to her apartment in Independent Living and playing bridge with us."

Charlie tugged at his collar and tie, clearly uncomfortable out of his usual tracksuit and running shoes. "That divorce was final ten years ago, but Rodney wouldn't let go. Wanted his trophy wife and Suzie too."

"Kept coming over," Alice said, "getting Suzie so upset, she'd have to take one of her pills." The former math professor studied each face. The friends seemed to be contemplating just where her words might lead.

Trudy adjusted her wire-rimmed spectacles. "Nearly worried Suzie to death."

"Bastard's lying," Fred repeated. The friends all looked at him, and Alice thought about how he was always irascible and frequently swore, but not like this. Fred might utter a "dammit" or a "SOB" but never words like "bastard." He must be really upset.

Charlie seemed to have lost patience with Fred. "Stop sounding like a broken record." He pointed at Rodney, standing across the room in the midst of a gaggle of admiring women.

No sign of his trophy wife, Alice noted. Maybe the second Mrs. Cunningham thought it would be bad taste to come? Or was it Rodney who decreed that she stay away?

"Of course, he's a liar," Charlie continued. "So what? Man lies at his wife's funeral. Wants everybody to think well of him. Rodney's been like that all his life."

"More to it than that," Alice said. "Remember what happened when Mary Margaret Gravesly died?"

Fred's voice was full of exasperation. "Obviously. We all went to that funeral too."

"Such a lovely lady," Trudy said. "Evergreen hasn't been the same since we lost Mary Margaret's volunteerism. She lived in that big mansion, yet she still had time for folks in need."

Fred tilted his head and squinted sideways at Charlie. "Whole slew of folks conspired to cover up *that* murder."

Their voices were getting too loud, and Alice raised both hands to bring the volume back down. "Eden and Bethanne got suspicious and teamed up to discover how Mary Margaret and Ray-Jean came to drown. Maybe someone ought to look into what happened to our friend."

Behind her spectacles, Trudy's eyes got big. "You-all mean to say you think Rodney killed Suzie?"

"Wouldn't put it past the SOB," Fred said.

Charlie stared at Fred, disbelief all over his face. "Gimme a break. What'd he do? Smother her with a pillow?"

Fred shrugged. "Bastard had a lot to gain."

Charlie sneered. "You watch too much TV. Oughta get out and exercise more."

Fred sneered back. "Great. Advice from a jock. Ever watch PBS? You might learn something."

Charlie was clearly ready to do something physical, and Trudy spoke up. "What do you mean, a lot to gain?"

Alice knew how much the six-time grandmother loved to snoop. She didn't want to go overboard replying to Trudy, but she did want to be responsive. "I think Fred's talking about Suzie's property. Big mansion and bigger farm. Been in the family for generations."

"Damn right I am," Fred said. "Maybe she lived with us at Evergreen and a while back with Rodney in that ultra-modern monstrosity on Country Club Drive, but Suzie held onto Great Oaks. Kept it so the kids and grandkids could use it on weekends. Swim in the pond. Fish in the creek. Run wild in the fields."

Trudy pushed her slipping spectacles back up. "Rodney dotes on his grandkids. Nothing he wouldn't do for them."

"Daughters'll get the estate," Charlie said. "Not Rodney."

"He spoiled those girls rotten," Fred said. "Especially that younger one. Always getting her out of scrapes."

"Wasn't there something about hitting her college roommate?" Trudy asked.

Fred nodded. "Cracked two teeth. Rodney had to go up there and fix things so she wasn't suspended. Whole thing was ruled an accident. Said Penelope took a swipe at the roommate and missed her. The girl lost her balance and fell against the bed. Rodney was always getting Penelope out of the messes she made. The other daughter too, but her messes weren't so many or so big." His eyes lit up. "Maybe he'll call in those chips to get that property."

Alice glanced across the hall to where Brenda and Penelope were talking with their father. "Rodney can be pretty persuasive when he wants to be," she said.

Later that afternoon, Alice sat on the sofa in her darkening apartment, stroking her ancient Siamese cat and thinking about her friends' reactions to Rodney's eulogy.

Her conscience tickled her, asking if she were running after a mystery that wasn't really there just to fill up the holes in her own life. She had to admit that since she'd retired from Lewiston Community College, she'd worked hard to discover something as challenging as teaching math and computer science. But she hadn't really found it.

She was no good at handwork like Trudy, so she couldn't get involved with the group that was always making seasonal decorations for the Evergreen dining room or bits and pieces for the annual Christmas Bazaar. Besides, if she were honest, Alice had to admit to herself that knitting and crocheting felt demeaning after a fulfilling professional life.

She'd enjoyed teaching an introductory computer course in the Evergreen Rec Room, but there hadn't been enough interest among the residents for a repeat.

The Evergreen Social Director had asked her to take over editing the residents' monthly newsletter. It didn't take long for that to become a burden. Repeatedly badgering volunteers to get their articles in on time had soon depressed her, and she'd made an excuse to give it up.

Many of the residents had children and grandchildren near. The families came to visit, or they took grandma or grandpa for an outing. Alice didn't have that, didn't want that. She'd never married and certainly never been the motherly type. In fact, when she ran into friends' grandchildren, she never knew what to say. She didn't want to go all goo-goo the way some residents did, but what do you say to a three year-old whose face is smeared with chocolate? For that matter, what do you say to the parents? No point in pretending to feelings she didn't have.

Alice stood up and stretched. Chow-Fan meowed in protest at being abandoned and slunk over to the kitchenette for a reassuring bite of kibble. Alice looked in the mirror above the brown-tweed sofa. She gazed at the cascade of African beads down her chest, wondering how she seemed to the other residents. The stereotypical old maid schoolteacher? With a cat to boot? Frumpy and eccentric? She shuddered. God forbid.

She came from a long-lived family. She'd likely live another twenty years or more. So what if she were looking for something challenging to do? What was wrong with that? Better than reading in an easy chair all day and playing bridge once a week. Besides, there was definitely something off about Rodney's eulogy. She wasn't making that up. Fred had seen it too, and Trudy's voice had carried a note of suspicion, though she was too well-bred to say so. Rodney wanted something. Enough to kill for it? Or had he just taken advantage of events?

Autumn's increasingly early evening dimmed the room now, but Alice clearly saw what she needed to do. She turned on a light against the gloom and smiled at her reflection. She had the beginning of a plan.

2

ALICE PUT HER PLAN INTO ACTION the next morning by inviting Suzie's bridge-playing friends over for tea in a few days. They were all somewhere in their seventies, and despite a few aches and pains, everyone was pretty mobile. They participated in a variety of activities on- and off-campus, driving here and there, meeting friends and family for meals, events and local excursions. Evergreen's Independent Living offered not only their own apartments. Residents also enjoyed a choice of one-to-three dining-room meals a day, little or no gardening as they desired, plus routine cleaning and washing of household linens once a week. Finally, there was the convenience of medical care on campus if and when they needed it. As Fred once put it, "At my age, where would I find it this good?"

When the invitation-day arrived, Alice closed Chow-Fan in the bedroom with litter box, water and a snack. The cat made her displeasure howlingly audible but soon calmed down. Alice's small living room was somewhat cramped for seven, but she pulled over two ladder-backed chairs from the dining alcove, so everyone could sit around the coffee table. With three people on the sofa and one in each of the beige-striped easy chairs, she hoped the set-up would feel cozy and inviting.

Everyone arrived almost at the same time, bubbling with energy and Evergreen gossip. Alice served tea or coffee while Trudy passed around a plate of store-bought cookies from Alice's cupboard. Once they were all settled, Alice steered the conversation to Suzie and Rodney.

"What good would Great Oaks do Rodney?" Willard asked. He heaved his bulk around the easy chair, but it didn't seem to fit. Alice felt a surge of sympathy for Willard. Ever since his wife died, he couldn't seem to stop stuffing food down. He must have gained fifty pounds.

The fat man continued, "You never saw a place farther from civilization. Rodney couldn't make a penny off it."

Alice shifted her gaze from Willard to George. A typical small-town lawyer, versed in a variety of legal subjects and widely respected, George had retired and moved from Moorestown to Evergreen. "What do you think?" she asked.

George put down his cup and crossed his long legs, showing a bit of argyle sock above his two-tone gray saddle shoes. His eyes wandered across her wall of books before he said, "Hard to say."

"Dammit, George," Fred said, "I never knew you to be anything but cautious. There's something to this, I tell you." He turned to Willard. "And you can't forget you used to be an accountant. Just because you can't see any money in it doesn't mean Rodney can't. You all should have been at the funeral. If you'd seen how that hypocrite behaved, you'd be suspicious too."

Trudy held up both hands in admonishment. "Not everyone feels comfortable at funerals, Fred. At our age, it can be too much of a reminder of things we don't want to think about." She rummaged through her oversized handbag and brought out tiny knitting needles with a baby's half-finished jacket.

When Trudy mentioned funerals, Alice noticed Charlie stealing his hand to pat her arm, just inches from his own as they sat together on the sofa. Trudy dipped one needle into a tiny loop of the knitting. Alice thought how Trudy always seemed like the image of what a grandmother should be, huggably plump and unfailingly sympathetic.

Willard clasped his hands over the rolls of fat on his sagging belly and stuck out his lower lip. "Follow the money, that's what I always say." He glared at Fred. "There's nothing out there except an old farm that hasn't produced a thing since Suzie was a girl. She kept up that big house, but she let the land go to waste."

Alice offered more cookies, but there were no takers. "Maybe it's not the farm or that beautiful old mansion," she said. "Maybe it's something else he wants."

Charlie unzipped his tracksuit jacket in the warm room. "Rodney wants everyone to think he's a great guy. Pure and simple."

"Well, he *is* a great guy," Anne-Marie said. "Used to play golf with my Tom." Her teal-blue eyes welled up, and everyone waited for the widow to finish. "Rodney never failed to buy a round of drinks when he won. Always gallant to the ladies and kind to the caddies."

Trudy nodded her silvery head. "That's true. That's true."

"Jesus," Fred said, "Rodney just acts that way because he thinks it'll help him get what he wants. Man's a goddam barracuda."

Alice prodded a bit more. "Yes, but what does he want?"

Fred's short, wiry body seemed to be bobbing in affirmation. "That's what we gotta find out, sister."

Everyone else sipped their tea and gazed through the sliding glass doors to the patio where Alice's potted mums were looking a bit worse for wear. Then Anne-Marie changed the subject to Evergreen's next scheduled guest lecture, and the topic of Rodney and Suzie drifted away.

Alice felt frustration balloon. This wasn't what she'd hoped for. Nobody but Fred seemed to share her suspicions. She thought back to the church hall. Well, maybe Trudy too, but she often said what she thought would make the last speaker feel good. Rodney's version of Suzie's death was definitely peculiar. If most of Suzie's friends couldn't appreciate that, there was nothing Alice could do to force them into action. On the other hand, did she really want to team up with Fred? The man was a loose cannon, too emotional to be effective and too foul-mouthed to be as delicate as the situation required. Perhaps she should let it ride for now. Maybe something would happen to bring everybody on board.

While Alice's living room was full of bridge friends, Eden was rushing around the corner of Evergreen's Skilled Nursing Facility with an armload of blankets. She literally ran into Jimmy Lee and Flossie. He grabbed Eden's elbows and kept her upright while Flossie sat down as she'd been trained to do.

"Whoa," Jimmy Lee said. "What's the hurry?"

Eden caught her breath. "Thanks. Just trying to work off some steam. Greg Pendergast is doing his best to take over the EverTeens' duties again. I cannot endure that man."

Jimmy Lee reached down to fondle Flossie's ears. The therapy dog had been visiting Evergreen residents for several weeks now. The institutional smell didn't seem to bother her anymore, but she still got anxious when the routine changed.

"Come on," he said to Eden. "We'll walk with you, and you can tell us all about it." Jimmy Lee started to move, and Flossie came immediately to his left side. He couldn't help but grin when the most sweet-tempered German Shepherd he'd ever raised was heeling nicely.

The President of the EverTeens smiled up at him. "You know how one of our duties is to read to residents..."

"Sorry to interrupt," Jimmy Lee said, "but I need to ask, how come they're called 'residents' and not 'patients?' Seems to me they're here because they need some kind of medical care or physical therapy. It makes sense the folks in Independent Living would be called 'residents.' But here, in Skilled Nursing and over in Assisted Living?"

Eden masked her annoyance at being interrupted by blowing a lock of brown hair out of her eyes. "They feel better about themselves and why they're here if they're called that." She tilted her head. "Now can I get back to what I was saying?" She waited for Jimmy Lee to nod and continued. "The adult Volunteers bring round the cart of books and magazines, and the EverTeens read to the residents if they ask us to. Pendergast can't stand that. He wants to read too. Just leaves the cart out in the hall and settles down to entertain the old folks."

"Tell Bethanne. She's in charge of adult Volunteers, right?"

"Yeah. She's Coordinator for all the Volunteers, adults *and* teens."

"So let her coordinate." He looked at Eden, still a bit pink in the face with emotion. "Want a Coke? I'm buying."

She smiled again, her color returning to normal. "Kind of you, but I got to get these blankets to the dining room. They're about to have a sing-along for the mobile residents, and some of them are cold-natured, always needing a little extra warmth."

Eden took a couple steps away and wheeled back. "If I'm going to be a doctor, I got to learn how to deal with in-house politics."

Jimmy Lee kept his mouth tightly shut, raised his eyebrows and nodded. That was true for sure. Eden had already changed a lot since they were boyfriend and girlfriend. And she was bound to change a lot more when she graduated this spring and headed off to the University.

She whirled around and was off down the hall. Jimmy Lee fondled Flossie's ears again and watched Eden's pell-mell dash. Yeah, a lot of changes since those days. Eden had been just starting high school. Now she was a senior. He'd been 16 and had to quit school to work when Dad died in the mine. He'd suffered through the losses of Miz Simmons and Lazarus, a dog whose life and death changed Jimmy Lee forever. That suffering led him to solve the mystery of who killed Miz Simmons and finally to start a kennel business with the inheritance she left him.

Jimmy Lee turned to resume the visits with the Skilled Nursing residents, and Flossie rotated with him. His thoughts turned also, to how he'd seen Greg Pendergast sneaking out of Suzie Cunningham's room in the days before she passed. The man's ego had to be pretty weak if he had to feed it with EverTeen duties.

Fred left the meeting in Alice's apartment seething with exasperation. Were they the only two people who could see Rodney for what he was? Dinner that evening with Suzie's friends at their usual Evergreen table only fed that frustration. Maybe no one else would do anything to nail Rodney, but he could. Fred needed action, any action. He went back to his place, put on old jeans, a dark sweat shirt and a navy cap to cover his thinning hair and shiny scalp. He snuck out his door, looking right and left, relieved to find nobody about at that hour.

Once outside, he trotted down the walk to his car and pulled out of the parking lot with headlights off so as not to call attention to his departure. When he got to the main road, he turned on the lights and drove carefully though town, still trying to avoid notice. It wasn't long before he was at the Lewistown Plaza, Rodney's pride and joy as a developer. The open-air shopping center had been built some years ago near the top of what had once been a hill of lush forest. Rodney had already made a killing from mining the underlying coal. Then he dynamited and bulldozed the acreage to make a huge flat space for no end of shops and restaurants, hotels and services. That late at night, everything but the hotels was closed. The empty parking lot, stretching for hundreds of yards, was lit by the harsh glow of mercury-vapor lights.

Initially, the buildings had been backed by raw, red clay, but nature had taken over and covered the abomination with vines and bushes. Fred drove to the supermarket at one end of a string of storefronts. Looking all around to make sure he wasn't being observed, he circled behind the market and under the vine-covered cliff. He parked his car in the deep shadow of a tree that had managed to hang on even though its topmost branches had sunk down to some eight feet above the asphalt. He got out and surveyed his surroundings. Thank God his car was navy, just like his clothes. It would take some pretty sharp eyes to spot his old Caddy.

He slipped away from the car as fast as he could, heading for the offices housed in the biggest building in the center of the Plaza. The front door to this complex faced the main parking lot, but there was also a small door that opened onto the back, where employees parked. Fred's dentistry clinic had once been one of the Plaza's services, and he'd come to Rodney's offices to select space and sign a lease. He'd hated having to move his clinic from downtown to up on the hill. But downtown was nearly empty once the shopping center was built, the hilltop location was convenient for his patients with lots of parking, so what the hell. "Can't fight progress," everyone had said. He'd learned to bear it, even if he couldn't grin about it.

Fred got to the back door of Rodney's office and looked for

an alarm company logo. No such warning anywhere. Was Rodney that dumb? The door was probably alarmed, even so. Didn't matter, because the staff bathroom was beside that door, and someone had left the window cracked, no doubt airing out the room. The window was high, but there was a wheeled garbage bin just a couple feet away. Metal with two lids of heavy-duty plastic. That ought to support his weight. Fred tried pushing the bin over, relieved to find it nowhere near full. Piece of cake. One of the lids was open. The other was down, so it was easy to climb onto the closed side and try the window. He patted his trim tummy and gave thanks he'd stayed in shape all these years.

Carefully he pushed at the window, only to discover it had one of those latches that allowed it to open two inches but no more. Damn! Should he break it? He pivoted to see a tempting rock at the base of the cliff. It was one thing to sneak in an open window but quite another to break that window. While he was standing there trying to make up his mind, he heard the unmistakable sound of a night watchman checking in via radio or walkie-talkie or whatever they used. Man was even saying, "10-4." Those guys definitely watched too much TV. Where the hell was the jerk? Inside or outside?

When a flashlight beam rounded the far end of the building, Fred knew there was only one thing to do. He eased down into the open side of the bin, trying to breathe through his mouth while holding his nose. Damn, it stunk like a week's worth of moldy lunches, soured milk and God-knew-what-else had been left to spoil in the autumn sun. But at least it was only a quarter-full, so he could hunker down out of sight. And one of the lids was open, letting a little cool night air into the stench. Even though Fred was inside the bin, he could tell from the changing glow that the rent-a-cop was coming closer and swinging his flashlight from side to side. Why the hell wasn't he in a car? Why was the stupid idiot on foot? Surely Rodney was too cheap to pay for foot-patrol security.

Now the guy was talking into his comm-device again. "Don't care what the boss saw on the surveillance cameras. Ain't nobody back here."

Shit, Fred thought. It hadn't occurred to him to watch out for cameras.

The guard was continuing, "You gonna come pick me up or what? You got the coffee? I don't like being on foot back here. Get the coffee and get here. Now." A scratchy voice sounded, too blurred for Fred to understand, and the nightwatchman said, "10-4. Meet you there." Gritty-sounding feet walked over to the bin, a hand appeared over the rim, and the open lid was slammed shut. The sound of the feet shifted back the way they'd come, and Fred was trapped in the biggest mess of his life.

3

ALICE COULDN'T SLEEP AFTER HER MEETING with Suzie's friends. She tried not to be upset. They were good people, but they just couldn't see things the way she did. On the morning Alice had visited, Suzie had said she was coming back to Independent Living the next day. By that afternoon, she was dead. It just didn't add up. If Suzie's friends weren't ready to face that, Alice would have to find another way to get them motivated.

For now, they'd only be together at meals, and the dining room was no place to talk about what had happened to Suzie. No one felt like playing bridge so soon after her death, but they were going to try again in a couple of weeks. That seemed like forever, but maybe it would be the next best chance to broach the topic again. Alice rolled over, still wide awake. Perhaps something else might happen before then. After a while, she sat up, turned on the light and picked up one of the books she'd borrowed from Evergreen's library. A mystery, that ought to do the trick. She'd get lost in that and let go of her gloom at the lack of a response.

Sunk in garbage up to his knees, Fred felt in his pockets for his key ring. What the hell was the matter with him? Why couldn't he find it? Getting old? Panicked by the dark and the stink? Finally, his fingers found it in a pocket he'd already searched. He brought it out and flicked on the tiny, attached flashlight he'd balked at buying when Willard had suggested it. Well, bless Willard now. His old buddy from high school days was right once in a while.

Fred shined the light up at the bin lids and tried to push one open, but the heavy plastic held firm. The overhanging edge had obviously caught on the metal bin's protruding rim, and it would take someone from outside to pry it up. Fred tried to bang a lid open, then kick it open, all without result. He almost threw his back out getting a foot up that high, even if he did lean back against the bin wall to steady himself.

He needed something to pry at a lid, but the bin only had leftover lunches and crap like that inside. He kicked at the rubbish, tossing it this way and that, trying to get down to the lowest level and hoping for something, anything, to get him out of this muck. Dammit, the flashlight was getting dim. Or maybe that was his eyes, trying so hard to focus in semidarkness.

He was starting to think about trying to phone Willard, despite all the grief he'd get, when his foot struck something hard. He reached down, pulled it out of the gunk and saw it was an old-fashioned carpet sweeper. He remembered seeing Rodney's cute, young secretary using one to sweep the rug around her desk when she'd upset a canister of shredded paper. At the time, he'd thought how some old-fashioned things could still be useful in a modern office. This one might be broken now, but it ought to fill the bill.

He unscrewed the metal rod from the sweeper's base and pushed it under the bin cover. Thank God for modern stuff too. The lid's heavy plastic felt pliable. It seemed to take forever, but Fred was finally able to push up enough of the lid that he could fit his wiry body through. When he was in high school and Willard played linebacker, Fred had felt sorry for himself that he wasn't built for sports. Well, Willard was fat now, and Fred could wiggle out of smelly garbage bins in the middle of the night. Maybe they should make that one of those ninja sports Charlie liked to watch on TV.

He laughed to himself about the idea as he headed for home, but then all that had happened hit him hard, and he started to shake. He'd been damn lucky. And stupid. What did he think he was going to find, anyway? Rodney surely kept anything important in a safe. And Fred was no more a safe-cracker than he was a second-story man. He'd gone off half-cocked because he was desperate for action to fight his frustration. He needed to ease back and think more about what else he could do.

He stole into Evergreen, thankful it was after midnight, so the Independent Living hallways were empty. Otherwise, somebody would've smelled him from yards away. Fred unlocked his apartment door and sidled through. He needed a hot shower. Time enough to clean his clothes and car in the morning.

It had taken a couple weeks, but Alice's plan for an investigation was moving forward. She'd gathered Suzie's friends in Evergreen's Game Room for a morning of bridge. The two weeks' hiatus seemed to be feeding their enthusiasm for a rousing game now. Hopefully, this would offer an opportunity to galvanize them into action.

"Two no-trump," came Willard's deep voice from the other table.

Alice waited for Fred to make a play at her table and looked around the homey room. Outside dripped one of fall's cold and dreary rains, but inside all was cozy and warm. The deep-blue carpet complemented the chintz curtains, sofas and chairs, plus the players had the pure joy of real-wood bridge tables and chairs. None of that rickety metal-and-vinyl stuff for Evergreen, thank goodness. The mild scent of lavender wafted from the furniture polish.

Over at Willard's table, he partnered Trudy while Anne-Marie put up with Charlie's usual inability to concentrate. Alice smiled across her own table at George, whose concentration was legendary. As a rule, he could repeat every hand played, in order, days later. They made a good pair. She couldn't stand partners who didn't come to play serious bridge. A Life Master herself, she'd had to learn to adapt to a different standard when she'd come to live at Evergreen, but that didn't mean she had to like it.

But today was different. She was hoping that Evergreen's awe-inspiring grapevine had stirred up more suspicion about Rodney.

On her right, Fred was looking back and forth from his cards to those displayed as a dummy before the empty seat opposite. He was a pretty good bridge player, even if it did take him a long time to make up his mind.

Alice's eyes lingered on Suzie's empty chair. The friends hadn't been able to bring themselves to consider inviting anyone else to join them just yet. They'd keep on playing a three-handed version until it felt right to find another bridge-player.

Fred finally selected a card from the dummy, and the game continued.

At the other table, Anne-Marie said, "Hear the latest? Brenda and Penelope are already fighting over Great Oaks. Three spades."

"Suzie not even cold in her grave," Trudy said. "Three no-trump."

Alice sucked in her lips. That sounded promising. What had Anne-Marie heard? She smiled across her own table at George and picked up their trick.

The gossip came to a halt, though, when Anne-Marie's partner, Charlie, was lost as usual. "What's the bid?" he asked.

Willard, across from Trudy, gave an exasperated sigh. "Three no-trump to you."

Their table's play continued, but at Alice's table, Fred took up the theme. "No surprise to me. Those kids got their mother's looks and their father's morals."

Trudy turned in her chair. "Shame on you, Fred. If you can't say anything nice, best not to say anything at all. Besides, it's Penelope who looks like her mother, not Brenda."

"Shut up and deal," Willard said.

Later, as they sat around their usual post-play nibbles, Alice maneuvered the subject back to Suzie's estate. "What's the trouble between Penelope and Brenda?"

Anne-Marie licked her plumped-up lips. "I heard it at the hairdressers." She lifted a hand to where an artful, silver-blond wave covered the thin scar in front of her ear." The sisters can't agree on what to do with the place. Brenda wants to buy Penelope out and move in just as soon as she can make it happen. Can't wait to spruce up the old mansion and live in all that history. But Penelope wants to turn it into a B&B. She'd run it and share the profits with Brenda."

"See?" Willard huffed. "It's always about money."

Alice tried not to react as he stuffed a whole chocolate cookie into his gaping mouth, crumbs cascading down his shirt. His jowly cheeks flapped to and fro as he chewed. "Well, not really, Willard," she said. "They both want to save the house. Brenda wants the prestige, and Penelope wants a new business. Maybe she's bored with her artificial-flower shop in Rodney's mall and wants a new challenge."

She turned to George. "How do they work this out legally? They both inherited, right?"

George uncrossed his legs and recrossed them in the other direction. Navy socks with white polka dots this time, Alice noted, color-coordinated with his navy cardigan and white shirt. George probably didn't know how not to be dapper.

"Had lunch with Suzie's lawyer the other day," he replied. "Farnsworth said she left everything to both equally. Easy to work out the legal part. One buys out the other. But hard to resolve it emotionally. They can't both be happy."

"No way Penelope could buy out Brenda," Willard said. "Three kids, husband a high school teacher, and she probably struggles just to break even with her flowers. That shop's more a hobby than a money-maker."

Charlie sat up straight. "What about mineral rights? Any coal or gas under that land?"

Wow, thought Alice, she'd never contemplated that. And maybe Charlie was coming on-board the quest.

"Might be worth looking into," Willard said. Alice thought she could kiss him, if it weren't for all those crumbs on his chest.

She turned her attention to George. "How do we find out? Would there be a record if somebody were on the prowl for minerals at Suzie's place?"

"Unlikely there are any mineral rights left to sell," he said. "All that was settled decades ago. End of nineteenth, early twentieth century. Shysters came in and bought up the rights before the landowners realized their true value." George folded his arms across his chest. "I can check it, just in case, but if you don't hear from me, there's nothing to it."

Charlie seemed deflated by George's recital, and Trudy looked up from her knitting to smile at the former coach.

Anne-Marie batted her eyelashes at George. *How obvious,* Alice thought, but then George was a lifelong bachelor and quite a catch. "Seemed like Suzie *was* short of cash," Anne-Marie was saying. "We used to go shopping or out to lunch all the time. But lately I'd invite her to go places, and she'd always say she couldn't afford it. She didn't act like that was going to change any time soon."

Fred raised his eyes to the ceiling like he was asking the Lord for patience. "What's that got to do with anything? We're talking about the daughters both wanting the place for different purposes. Besides, Rodney's the one who's acting suspicious. We just gotta find the connection."

Alice tried to make her voice soothing. "Fair enough, Fred. But what if Suzie were borrowing money from Rodney?" She turned to George. "And using her farm as collateral? Or the mineral rights?"

George wagged his well-groomed head back and forth. "As I said, probably no mineral rights there. But the land might have some value. Lot of development around here nowadays."

"See?" Willard repeated. "Money. It's always about money."

Alice smiled to herself. What a difference fourteen days can make. Maybe now she could get some action.

That same morning, Bethanne sat behind a table on the dais of Evergreen's Rec Room, watching the assembled Volunteers fill up the folding chairs. Just the adult Auxiliary and the EverTeens, all from outside the Retirement Community. No need to bring in the residents who ran their own activities.

This kind of thing was her least favorite part of being the Evergreen Volunteer Coordinator. She'd learned a lot about handling conflict since the days when stress sent her to the bottle and a bender. AA had helped and so had support from friends like her business partner, Mae, and Eden's mother, Corrine. Perhaps most of all, she didn't want to disappoint Eden. To Bethanne's chagrin, the teenager had sobered her up more than once.

Bethanne nodded to herself. Her coping skills had been hard-won during her fifties. Now past sixty, she didn't like using those skills if she could avoid it.

The adult Volunteers were spread throughout the chairs, drinking coffee and chatting. Most wore light gray cotton tabards with the Evergreen logo, ready to start work as soon as the meeting was over. The EverTeens grouped together, looking like there was strength in numbers. Word must have got out about today's topic. They seemed apprehensive, like it was the fourth quarter and up to the kicker to save the game.

The Volunteer Coordinator regarded Eden sitting in the front row and wearing her light gray EverTeen pinafore. Happily, Bethanne's young friend had won early admission to study Pre-Med at the University. Now she seemed determined to make the most of this volunteer activity in the hopes of winning a scholarship too. But sometimes Eden took the EverTeens and herself just a little too seriously.

It looked like everyone was here, so time to get started. No one liked coming to a Saturday morning meeting, so Bethanne needed to make it short and to the point. But also handle it right, so everyone would get with the program and no hard feelings. She took in a slow breath to keep calm and let it out just as slowly.

The subdued chit-chat dwindled when she rose and walked to the front of the table. "Hi, everybody and welcome. I appreciate your coming. Did everybody get something to drink and a doughnut?" Heads nodded, and hands raised cups and glasses. An adult latecomer hustled to the refreshment table, grabbed her goodies and sat down in the back.

Bethanne smiled and leaned against her own table, hoping to set an informal tone. "I know you all have commitments, so I'll keep this as brief as possible." Some faces were smiling back. That appeared promising. "Let's start by welcoming our new adult Volunteers. Would you stand please?" Bethanne led the applause for the five newcomers. "We've ordered new tabards, but in the meantime, we only have just enough. No way to replace a ruined one. So take good care of them for a few weeks, okay?"

She paused. "Let me repeat something I've said before — how much the residents, staff and Board appreciate everything the Volunteers do to help keep Evergreen running smoothly. I really believe we couldn't do without you."

Now more faces were smiling. Time to deliver the main message. "But we've got a little loose about the duties of our two groups." Bethanne smiled again. "Probably wouldn't hurt to review those real quick, especially now we're about to start a new round with some new Volunteers."

She raised a clipboard, studied her talking points and briefly reviewed how residents in Independent Living wanted and needed to manage their own volunteer activities.

"Hear, hear," one of the Auxiliary women said. "My mother's

in Independent Living, and she'd read me the riot act if somebody implied she couldn't make change in their gift shop. Even if it does take her longer than it did a few years ago."

Several heads nodded, and one of the men said, "So where's the beef?"

"Not really a beef," Bethanne said. "Just a reminder. The Adult Auxiliary is doing a great job of staffing the Information Desk in the building that houses Assisted Living and Skilled Nursing." She smiled. "And running the Gift Shop there. The things you have for sale are right on target. Reading materials, cards, bud vases, candy, small mementos, they're all good."

Eden was tapping her foot on the floor, and Bethanne felt her own anxiety rise. She had to head Eden off at the pass. "I think where we may have a little snag is with the gift cart the Auxiliary takes around to the residents' rooms." Some of the Auxiliary members started to frown, and Bethanne rushed on, feeling caught in the middle. "Residents love buying themselves little treats when they can, and that cart has just what they want."

"So?" said the man who was pushing about the beef.

Bethanne tried not to squirm and to keep her voice warm. "We need to remember that it's important to get the cart around to *all* the residents. It's good to chat some and brighten someone's day. But if they buy a book or magazine and then want someone to read to them, that's an EverTeen job."

She did her best not to look at Eden or Greg, but she couldn't help noticing the EverTeen President turning around to smirk at him.

"Okay," said the beef man, "whoever's stepping on toes, do us all a favor and stop. Then we won't have to come to these damned meetings. Get some work done instead."

"Good idea," Bethanne said. "Let's all get to work."

Everyone filed out, Greg near the front. Eden came up to Bethanne and waited until they were alone. Bethanne smiled at her young friend and hoped for the best.

"Why didn't you name Pendergast for stepping over the line?" Eden asked. "All that soft talk will just go over his head."

Bethanne was careful to treat her like an adult. "I understand what you're saying. But you're heading up the EverTeens, and you know you can't push Volunteers. They have to want to do what's right. Let's wait and see what happens."

"Humph," said Eden and walked out.

Bethanne clutched her clipboard and took in another long breath. This one came out ragged with the tension she'd held inside. Okay, she was better at running meetings than she used to be. But how could she help Eden learn the patience she'd always lacked?

ALICE STOOD BY HER WINDOW, taking in the wet landscape. It'd been raining ever since their bridge game a couple of days before, and she'd been content to let her friends ponder their discussion. But now it was time to do a little prodding. She phoned George and gently pulled Chow-Fan's tail while he reviewed all the plays at their table for five minutes.

Then she changed the subject. "I got to thinking about Suzie needing money and the value you speculated Great Oaks might have. How do we find out if there's anyone planning some development out there?"

She could hear George's smile in his voice. "I was just making conversation," he said. "Suzie's estate is so far from town I can't imagine anyone would want to build on it."

"What about another country club?" she asked. "There hasn't been a new one in fifty years, and lots of new folks have come to town, what with the Community College expansion, the new federal tax facility and the gas company merger."

"Young folks aren't interested in golf these days. Too busy to learn a difficult game that takes four hours to play. They want family activities."

Alice watched the sun trying to push through the rain clouds. "Yes, but country clubs offer all kinds of family activities these days. I read about it in the *New York Times*. Not just swimming pools and tennis courts like before, but climbing walls and rope courses and even kicking soccer balls around a special circuit."

"Alice," George said, his voice sounding overly patient, "you're looking for something that's not there. If any such development were in the works, I'd have heard about it. Even if I'm retired and no longer in the pipeline, Farnsworth would've heard. He didn't say a word about a country club, and we talked a lot about property development in this county." He paused. "Oh, and I checked. No mineral rights left on Great Oaks land."

"Fap!" said Alice when they'd hung up.

A little rain didn't deter Bethanne and Mae from their weekly lunch at the Corner Cafe. Usually, they took turns keeping Gifts-n-Such open during the noon hour, but they'd learned they needed time to be together as friends, not just business partners.

They'd become so close, it felt like they'd been friends for decades. But it'd only been a few years since Mae had kept house for Bethanne's sister, who'd drowned with Eden's best friend. While Bethanne and Eden were investigating what happened, it slowly dawned on the woman raised in Alabama that the "colored maid," as she used to think of Mae, had become her friend. In the end, they put together their money to open Gifts-n-Such. The shop was a turning point in both their lives, and they rarely looked back.

They were talking about Mae's husband finding a job that was feasible with his maimed hand, when Rodney Cunningham walked in with his two daughters. The three nodded at the two women, then sat in the booth just behind Mae.

Bethanne's friend swallowed her mouthful of chili and said, "Jim doesn't need to use that hand except to steady things, and his supervisor already said if he keeps up the good work, there'll be a raise pretty soon. We can always use more money, what with an unexpected grandchild." She pulled out a picture of a baby. "That's the outfit you gave her for her first birthday."

Bethanne smiled and tried not to show her twinge of envy. She'd been married three times, but none of them had worked out. No kids and no grandkids either. "You're so lucky to have such a beautiful granddaughter," she said.

"Don't I know it?"

They talked at some length about Bethanne's duties as Volunteer Coordinator at Evergreen. Bethanne was feeling guilty about taking half-days off from Gifts-n-Such.

"So what do you think is more important?" Mae asked. "Selling stuff or helping sick folks?" Bethanne opened her mouth to reply, but Mae went on. "Besides, we both know Gifts-n-Such doesn't generate enough cash yet. We need you to have that part-time job. Don't worry. I can take care of the shop while you're at Evergreen. Then when it's your turn, I can run errands or whatever."

Bethanne still had something to say, but raised voices from the next booth butted in. From where she was sitting, Bethanne could see the back of Rodney's head and his daughters' faces opposite.

"No, Dad," Brenda said, "We don't want you to buy us out."

"Mom's place has been in the family for generations," Penelope added, her voice starting to break. "We have to keep it that way."

"What if I bought just the land and left you two the house? With five acres or so for privacy?" Rodney asked.

Brenda huffed. "That still doesn't solve the problem of

whether my family lives there, or Penelope turns it into a B&B."

Penelope started to speak, but Brenda continued, "Mother would turn over in her grave if she knew strangers were sleeping in her house."

The younger sister blushed, and her jaw clenched. Her voice turned spiteful. "She can't turn over in her grave. Daddy had her cremated."

Bethanne saw Rodney spring up and grab the check. "Well, you girls think it over. I gotta run."

Mae leaned across the table and whispered to Bethanne, "Why'd he have her cremated? I used to babysit for the Cunninghams. They're old-fashioned Baptists. Can't be resurrected if you don't have a body to raise up."

"Is that true?" Bethanne said. "Awful lot of folks getting cremated these days."

It'd been raining for the better part of a week. Charlie felt so cooped up, he was ready to shout for joy when the sun finally came out the next morning. He pulled on his elastic knee supports, double-tied his old running shoes and headed for the municipal park's track. He jogged the four blocks at his usual pace, fast enough to get his heart beating, slow enough to suit his bad knees.

When he got there, it looked like he wasn't the only one in need of a little exercise. Half of Lewiston must've had the same idea. Young professionals running like they were in a track meet, guys and gals both. Old duffers like him. And everything in-between. The young folks had on shorts and t-shirts with sweatshirts or jackets tied around the waist. Most people had on some kind of pants and jacket against the fall chill, usually in dull colors, but across the track, a woman in bright pink stood out. She had a pretty good stride, just wasting energy by tossing her blond mane back and forth. Kind of intriguing, so Charlie decided to wait until she came near.

His jaw almost dropped. The gal was Janice Cunningham, Rodney's trophy wife, and she was showing off how she got the title. Her pink velour tracksuit was skin-tight, the jacket unzipped to show cleavage pushed together by a matching sports bra. Her running shoes must've cost two hundred dollars.

Charlie was starting to get cold, so he slipped in behind her and tried to keep up. Janice was thirty-five, thirty years younger than Rodney and half Charlie's age. Still, he succeeded in matching her pace, secretly enjoying the bounce of her bum under that tight pink velour. *Dirty old man*, he tried to tell himself, but what harm did looking do? That's about all he had left these days.

Then he thought of Trudy and felt ashamed. She was twice the woman Janice was, three times, even. Trudy probably thought of him as just a friend, but he wished they could be more than that. Maybe they could, one day. It'd been a long time since his wife jumped ship. He needed someone to love. Charlie left the track and headed back to Evergreen, trying to be as good a man as Trudy was a woman.

While Charlie was running around in circles, Bethanne was standing at the junction of Evergreen's Assisted Living and Skilled Nursing facilities. She smiled as she reviewed the Volunteer sign-in sheet on the Information Desk. No absences and no latecomers for weeks now. Such lackadaisical behavior had been a problem when Bethanne had come on-board as Volunteer Coordinator, but she'd handled it with a light reminder, and folks had shaped up. Just like she'd done with the question of who reads to residents. Hopefully, that problem would be now resolved as easily.

The double doors to the outside sprang open, and she glanced up. Alejandro entered with a small basket of flowers in each hand. The delivery man from Blossoms Aplenty was a near-daily visitor to Evergreen. There was no need for him to sign the Guest Register required for most people who came from outside.

"Hello, Missis Swanson," he said with a smile.

"Those for me?" she teased.

His accent was warmed by the beaming smile. "Oh, I wish, but not this time." He turned to the Information Desk and asked the Volunteer for the room numbers of a couple transfers from Independent to Assisted Living.

Trudy Graham was volunteering today, always sharp and on-the-ball, despite her grandmotherly appearance. Trudy was one of the few Evergreen residents from Independent Living to volunteer for this facility. Most didn't seem to want to be reminded they might be here one day.

Bethanne waved at the two of them, put down the sign-in sheet and headed along the Assisted Living hallway to check out the chair-exercise class. There was a new Volunteer assisting the physical therapist, and Bethanne wanted to see how she was doing.

She watched the action for a few minutes, pleased to see the Volunteer encouraging the residents at the back as they lifted their knees and swung their arms. Keeping residents as mobile and strong as possible was one key to their well-being. The Volunteer had just the right touch, not pushing but trying to make the whole thing fun.

The building was actually a triangle with a garden in the

middle. The Skilled Nursing and Assisted Living wings were in a V-shape, joined by a third hallway, used for spillover when the other rooms were full. This was especially necessary when residents from outside Evergreen were accommodated on an as-needed basis. Right now, there was only one room in use on the Assisted Living end of the third hallway, so Bethanne used that route as a short-cut to Skilled Nursing.

She hurried past dark and empty rooms, heading for the lights of the Nursing wing. As she neared the end of the hallway, she heard voices coming from the last room in the row. The voices slipped through the crevice of open door, almost whispering, the tone both confidential and urgent.

"I think I should tell Missis Swanson," said a male voice. "She would know what to do."

Bethanne ducked into a shallow alcove and froze.

"No, Alejandro," said a female. "Don't risk it. Listen to me. I'm your big sister, and I know what I'm talking about."

"But I know I can trust her," came the voice she now knew belonged to the florist delivery man.

"No, you can't trust no one. You got too much to lose."

Oh Lord, thought Bethanne, *what do I do now?*

5

OVER IN THE GAME ROOM, Alice felt her pent-up breath escape. It had taken a lot of work to organize this bridge game in memory of Suzie. Now it was finally over, and she could get to the real purpose of the afternoon. She wondered if she should feel guilty about her hidden intentions but decided it was for all for their lost friend, one way or the other.

Alice had carefully pushed the idea of a memorial bridge game after the group's table talk at their first game after Suzie's funeral. She'd suggested they invite Penelope first, then Brenda, to take their mother's place for an afternoon. Penelope, Alice figured, was more likely to be forthcoming than her older sister.

Everyone agreed a couple of memorial bridge games would be a good idea except for Anne-Marie. "Oh gosh," she said, flickering her eyes at George, "Maybe it's too soon to invite Penelope to play with us. It might be too sad for her." But George said he liked the idea, and that turned Anne-Marie around.

Now they were all sitting on the chintz couches after the game, waiting for the sweet Alice had ordered and paid for herself. She cut a piece of the spice cake, put it on a plate and passed it to Penelope. "We have such happy memories of the time your mother invited us to play at Great Oaks," she said. "That was surely a special day."

Penelope wiped a smear of cream-cheese frosting from bright coral lips with her napkin. "Momma always was generous that way. Nothing she liked more than sharing Great Oaks with folks she cared about. I feel the same way." She paused. "In fact, I'd like to share that special place with the whole world."

Her green eyes got all shiny. "Don't know what will happen now. The kids really count on going out there every weekend when the weather's good." She tried to swallow, but it seemed difficult. "Me too. I don't think anybody really understands how much Great Oaks means to me."

Maybe Anne-Marie had been against inviting Penelope before, but she was true to her passion for gossip now. "I heard your Daddy wanted to buy you and Brenda out," she said.

Penelope bit her lips and glanced at the door. Alice thought she looked like escape was the perfect plan, if only she could bring it off.

"It must be hard for you," Alice said, "the house meaning so much."

"Well, Daddy just wants the land. He'd pay Brenda and me fair value, and then one of us could buy the other out."

"What's he want the land for?" Willard butted in. "No use to anybody."

Alice gave him a look that might kill, but he was totally oblivious to how he was rushing things. She tried another tack, "More cake, Willard?" He reached out eagerly for the giant piece she cut and settled down to eat the icing first.

She turned back to Penelope. "How will you and Brenda settle what to do about the house?"

"Flip a coin?" Fred suggested, and Penelope's mouth sagged open.

Trudy held up her hand, "That's enough, Fred. We didn't invite Penelope here to make silly suggestions."

But we did invite her here to get information, Alice thought and wondered who Trudy was trying to fool when she made such comments. The grandmother loved pulling off a good snoop, even if she couldn't admit it to herself or others.

Fred started to continue, but Charlie spoke up. "Saw your stepmother at the track this morning. Sure keeps herself fit."

Penelope gave him a tight little smile and a tighter nod. Alice was in despair. This turn of events was not what she had envisioned at all. Doggone these guys. They were going to ruin everything.

George saved the day. "Penelope, maybe you should consult with Sam Farnsworth about how all this might be best managed. Lot of issues involved."

She seemed relieved to move to a safer topic. "Thanks, Mr. Martino. He always gives such thoughtful advice. Mr. Farnsworth is a great problem-solver."

Alice didn't want to risk any more faux pas, so she steered the topic away from Great Oaks until the group broke up. Then she took Penelope by the arm and talked about missing her mother until everyone left. "We're all so concerned about what's going to happen to Great Oaks. It meant the world to Suzie."

Penelope blinked fast, again and again. "I just gotta have that house. Don't think I can live without it." She shook her head as if to clear it. "Maybe I shouldn't say this, but Daddy seems to think there's going to be some real estate development out that way and he could cash in for all of us." She smiled. "Daddy's always been so generous when I needed help in the past. Maybe he could give me some extra help now. He knows how much I want that B&B." Her eyes seemed to crinkle with pleasure. "And a petting zoo too. That would bring in even more income."

Alice walked Penelope out to her Nissan Pathfinder. The perfect car for a mom with three kids, she thought, looking into back seats loaded with piles of athletic equipment, fast food wrappers and a solitary hair ribbon. As Penelope drove away in a cloud of dust drifting off her chocolate-brown SUV, Alice was thinking about what the young woman had said. And what Alice's own friends had said at the funeral. Sure seemed liked Suzie's daughter was a Daddy's girl.

That afternoon, Bethanne sat with Mae over a cup of tea and her friend's home-made brownies. They'd closed up Gifts-n-Such and were enjoying an after-work chat in the back room.

Except Bethanne wasn't enjoying it, because she still had Alejandro on her mind. "I need to ask your advice," she said and relayed what had happened that morning.

"He wanted to tell you something because he trusts you," Mae said. "So make it easy for him. Order some flowers to be delivered here. I'll make myself scarce, and you can gently bring him around."

Bethanne grimaced. "*Gently* is not a word that applies to me."

Mae patted her arm. "Maybe not a few years ago. You were kind of a bull in a china shop when you first came to Lewiston." Bethanne nodded at the truth in Mae's words as her friend continued, "But that's not true now. Look how well you handle those Volunteers at Evergreen."

"Well..." Bethanne said as she thought about how far she'd come. She *was* starting to lead gently. Maybe she could do that with Alejandro.

Trudy sat at her worktable in the spare bedroom. She was sorting cotton scraps for the Christmas quilt she would donate to the yearly Church auction that raised money for the homeless. She liked to keep busy. "Idle hands are the Devil's playground," Grammy used to say. Besides, these tasks had helped Trudy build a new life since her husband had passed. Years ago, but sometimes it felt like yesterday.

She did have the comfort of her daughter and family. Sandy was still in the area, came by to visit, often bringing the kids, and took her out to lunch now and then. But Ed Junior was far away, an investment banker in Geneva. Trudy sighed, trying to look on the bright side. Ed's two sons were tri-lingual in English, German and French. That had to be a good thing, she reflected, the way the world was shrinking. And there was a baby on the way. The little knit jacket was almost finished. A smile came to light her face. Soon she'd have the blessing of seven grandchildren.

Trudy rotated her shoulders, the pain and stiffness more acute this evening, even though polymyalgia rheumatica was supposed to be worse in the morning and then slack off as the day wore on. At least that's what her rheumatologist said. Anyway, PMR wasn't the end of the world. She just had to accept it, work with it and keep taking her prednisone.

Maybe her tension over what she'd heard that morning was causing the pain. Trudy had come to the spare linen closet to get another pillow case for that poor Mr. Dent who'd thrown up all over his. The closet bulb was out, and she was standing in the dark when the whole thing happened. She didn't know whether to get involved or not. In a way, it had nothing to do with her. It was between that nice delivery man and his sister. But Trudy had seen

Bethanne lurking outside the room where they were talking. Should she speak to Bethanne? She didn't want Alejandro to get in trouble with Evergreen. But she also didn't want Bethanne to think she'd been snooping. All so embarrassing and yet important.

Trudy clasped her hands in prayer, asking the Lord for guidance. And the answer came. Do nothing now. Wait and see if something is needed. Trudy sighed, turned out the light and headed for bed.

Suzie's friends were at their usual lunch table a couple days later, when Alice looked up and saw Willard and Fred bursting into the Evergreen dining room. Willard's shirt was flapping around his belly, and Fred was literally foaming at the mouth.

The two men rushed past the hostess and fell into their chairs, one on either side of Alice.

Fred grabbed a napkin to wipe the spittle from his mouth as Willard panted, "I knew it! What did I say? Always about the money."

Willard stopped to drink half his glass of water in one swig, and Fred jumped in, "I told you Rodney's a prize bastard. Saw that from the get-go. Wait'll you hear what we found out." His triumphant voice bounded around the dining room.

Alice saw just about every face in the room whip its focus to the two men. Heads turned. Bodies leaned. It was as if almost everyone wanted to listen in.

She put a hand on each man's arm and applied a little soft pressure. "You're absolutely right," she said in a low voice. "We can hardly wait to hear what you have to say." She gestured with her chin at the other diners. "But let's wait until we get back to my place."

The two men glanced around, and Willard appeared chagrined. But Fred shook his head. "Don't give a good goddam. This can't wait."

Willard's glower could have stopped a wild bull, let alone Fred. "Oh, yes, it can." He surveyed their table, and Alice saw all eyes were on him. Even Anne-Marie's, who usually couldn't take her orbs off George. "But you're not going to believe it," Willard said.

Across town, Jimmy Lee and Eden were having a Coke at Quik Treet, before she went to volunteer at Evergreen. They still met now and then to nurture their friendship and stay in touch.

"Don't hear you complaining about Greg Pendergast no more," Jimmy Lee said. "That all over?"

Eden wrinkled her nose. "At least for now. Looks like Bethanne was right to handle it low-key."

"A lesson there?" he asked.

"Maybe, but part of me is still wondering."

"How come?"

Eden squirmed in her chair. "Once Miz Suzie passed, Pendergast went back to pushing the cart around, selling something and moving on. I was so ticked at him, I didn't realize he'd stopped reading to residents before Bethanne talked to the Volunteers. And then I realized he wasn't reading to everyone, just to Miz Suzie."

He grinned. "You sure have a suspicious streak, Eden Jones." She started to rise to the bait, but he continued. "Fact is, I was puzzling over that myself. I saw Pendergast leaving Miz Cunningham's room more'n once. It was always like he was sneaking out, not just walking away after selling her a magazine or whatever."

Eden sat up straight and gazed into Jimmy Lee's eyes. "So what was going on?"

He looked back just as directly and said, "Dunno, but maybe we better find out."

Eden smiled, and her eyes twinkled. "No point bothering Bethanne or the Evergreen Director with this 'til we have something concrete."

6

"So Willard has this accountant friend at the County Planning Commission," Fred said, smirking from ear to ear. "And we really got the low-down."

Alice could hardly contain herself. She observed Suzie's friends, scattered around her living room, and they looked like she felt. Thank goodness Chow-Fan was closed up in the bedroom again. Otherwise, she'd pick up on the excitement and ricochet, yowling, around the room.

Willard raised both big hands in the air. "Let me tell it. I'm the one set it up. You just tagged along."

"No I didn't. You wanted me for a witness." Fred started to rise, hands on knees and red in the face.

"Hold on," George said. "Let's everybody calm down. Willard, you first. Then Fred, if he has something to add."

"Or correct," Fred growled, but he sat down and leaned back.

Willard took a gulp of the water Alice had provided. "Okay. I got this friend from college who works at the County Planning Commission. Figured he might know something, so I invited him for a drink yesterday evening and had Fred come along in case we needed two sets of ears and eyes."

"See?" Fred said, his voice full of satisfaction.

"Shut up, Fred," Charlie said. "Let Willard tell it. You'll get your chance."

Fred ground his teeth, but he kept quiet.

Willard blushed and rubbed his chin. "I knew this guy had a little problem with alcohol, so I kept buying drinks 'til he was loosened up."

Not very ethical, Alice thought, but it was too late now.

"Then ol' Willard went in for the kill," Fred said. "I was about half-tanked myself."

George gave Fred the kind of expression he must have used in the courtroom to great effect. Fred nodded once, hung his head and looked up at George.

It was all Alice could do not to prompt Willard herself.

The big man wiped his face, shook his head and eyed his assembled friends. "There's going to be an exit for that new highway right near Suzie's property. Great Oaks'll be worth millions."

While Willard and Fred were telling all in Alice's living room, Bethanne was waiting anxiously at Gifts-n-Such for Alejandro to deliver the flowers she'd ordered. Mae had gone out to the bank to deposit the shop's earnings, so Bethanne could be alone with him.

Bethanne kept looking past the window display for the Blossoms Aplenty van. She still didn't have a plan, and that made her nervous. Bethanne walked to the rear of the shop so Alejandro wouldn't see her looking out the window. She began rearranging a table of china gnomes, just to have something to do with her hands.

What could she say to get Alejandro to talk? She didn't want him to know she'd been eavesdropping in the Evergreen hallway.

Especially with his sister letting it slip he had too much to lose. What did that mean? Was he an illegal alien? That didn't matter to Bethanne. She was the descendent of an illegal alien who'd stowed away on a ship just before the First World War. Besides, Alejandro was as hard-working and ethical as any citizen. Even more than some Lewiston folks she knew. Maybe he'd come here to escape hardship and poverty just like her own ancestor. But if he knew Bethanne had heard what his sister said, no way he'd open up.

The tinkle of the old-fashioned bell on the shop door whipped her around to face her lack of a plan.

"Hi, Missis Swanson. Sorry it took me awhile. I was loaded up with flowers for a funeral and a baby shower that had to be delivered first." Alejandro gestured with a vase of flowers. "This had to be last. Hate to keep you waiting."

He seemed older than she'd thought. He'd struck her like a guy around twenty. Now he seemed more like thirty. Bethanne tried to make her smile reassuring. "Not at all. Got time for a cup of coffee? I was just going to get one myself."

Alejandro looked at the clock above Bethanne's head. "I need to get back to Blossoms Aplenty before it closes, but yeah, I got five minutes." He grinned. "Maybe even ten."

She opened the brightly flowered curtains to the back room, quickly poured two mugs from the pot there and returned to the shop. Alejandro was still standing with the vase of flowers. *Dope*, she told herself, *your nerves are messing you up.*

"Oh, Alejandro," she said, "I'm sorry, I was in such a hurry to get your coffee that I forgot those beautiful flowers." She put the mugs down on a counter, took the flowers and placed them in the center of the table with the gnomes and realized she'd forgotten what went with the coffee. She had to get hold of herself or risk losing this chance. "How about milk or sugar?" she asked.

He seemed to be a little off now himself. His hands were jammed in the pockets of his green Blossoms Aplenty jacket, and his face was stiff. Her lack of ease was probably affecting him too. "Ah...both," he said and looked everywhere but at her.

Bethanne dashed back for the packets of powdered creamer and sugar they kept in the back room, collected two spoons and hurried through the open curtains with another smile. "Don't know what's the matter with me today. Can't seem to remember anything. Must be getting old."

Alejandro smiled back. "Not you, Missis Swanson. You'll always be young at heart, and that's what counts."

She pulled a couple stools out from behind the counter and offered one to him. "Blossoms sure keeps you busy."

He stirred in two packets each of creamer and sugar. "Can't be too much work for me. I'm grateful for the job."

Getting too close to his being an illegal alien? she wondered and decided to take a different tack. "Folks at Evergreen sure are grateful for you." Alejandro sipped his coffee while she continued, "I wanted to ask your advice. You see things I don't at Evergreen. It feels to me like maybe something's going on there, but I can't put my finger on it."

His eyes opened wide, and his chin jutted forward a fraction.

Was she going too fast? Too late now, Bethanne thought, she had to keep going. She inclined her head and lowered her voice. "Just between us, you ever see anything fishy?"

"Fishy?" he asked.

"Yeah, something that doesn't seem right."

Alejandro took another drink of coffee, swallowing hard. He

looked to the right of her, then to the left, then up at the clock. He opened his mouth, then closed it again. Finally, he took a breath to speak.

Just as Mae came through the back door. It was clear he could see her through the open curtains. He glanced up at the clock again. "Uh-oh, getting late. Gotta get back to Blossoms. Thanks for the coffee."

And there was nothing Bethanne could do to keep him from bolting.

Meanwhile, Fred was gloating to Suzie's friends. "Told you Rodney was lying. He killed Suzie to get his hands on her land. Gonna make himself a billionaire."

"Hold on," George said, "Suzie left everything to her girls."

Alice watched Anne-Marie look at George and nod her head like he'd said something profound.

Willard leaped in to say what Alice was thinking. "Yeah, but Penelope already told us he wants to buy 'em out." Now Alice was the one nodding.

Fred added, "Probably kill them too, if he has to."

Alice's nodding turned to shaking her head. "Come on, that's going too far. You found all this out yesterday?"

Willard looked sheepish. "Yep."

She tried to keep him from seeing how upset she was. "So why didn't you tell us then?"

Fred snickered. "Willard was three sheets in the wind."

"Well, you were four," the big man retorted. Then he looked even more sheepish. "We had to sleep it off."

Fred interrupted, "We were gonna just take a little nap and tell you at dinner. But we didn't wake up 'til this morning."

"Oh Fred," Trudy said, "you know you're not supposed to drink alcohol with your meds."

Charlie sat up straight in Alice's beige-striped chair. "I know I've been holding out, but I'm convinced now. What do we do?"

"Catch the bastard," Fred said.

George's expression turned skeptical, but Alice saw her opening, the opening she'd been hoping for since the day she'd first formulated her plan. "Each of us has know-how. Put them all together, and we've got everything we need."

"Yeah," Charlie said. "We'll be a team." He grinned. "A winning team. What do we call ourselves?"

"The Silver Foxes," Anne-Marie said, looking thrilled with herself.

George eyed all the gray heads."Not at all sure this is a good idea. But we've sure got the hair for it."

Alice felt every bit as thrilled as Anne-Marie looked.

EDEN COULD BARELY SIT STILL through her classes at Lewiston High. She tried to concentrate in Calculus. The University scholarships wouldn't be awarded until the spring, and she needed an "A" in Calculus as further proof of what a dedicated student she was. But her mind kept drifting to the plan she and Jimmy Lee had devised the day before, when they were at Quik Treet. Thank goodness he'd agreed to look into Pendergast's suspicious behavior with Miz Suzie.

Finally school was out, and she ran down the steps to where Jimmy Lee was waiting in his beige Chevy Suburban with "Good Shepherd Kennel" on the sides. "You sure look pretty with your face all flushed like that," he said, "but maybe you need to calm down some before we get to Evergreen?"

Eden gave him a lop-sided grin and climbed into the passenger seat. "I'll be fine by the time we get there. Have some faith."

Flossie had been lying in the back of the SUV. Now she came forward, and Eden began massaging the dog's ears. The German Shepherd groaned with pleasure.

Eden looked at Jimmy Lee and shook her head. "No need for you to be watching over me."

Jimmy Lee drove to the retirement community while they

reviewed their plan. Eden hopped down, grabbed her books and ran inside while he parked the SUV, made sure Flossie's "Therapy Dog" vest was on right and attached the lead to her collar.

Then he and Flossie went into Assisted Living for their visitation rounds. They started in the dining room, where the daily bingo game was in session. Despite the players' intense concentration, there were several waves to master and dog as the tiles were slapped down. Shortly someone shouted, "Bingo!" and the leader called a break. Jimmy Lee brought Flossie forward, and they got their usual warm welcome. The residents seemed starved for a friendly dog's attention, and Flossie didn't let them down, sitting patiently while they patted her head, stroked her coat and told her how beautiful she was.

That was true, Jimmy Lee reflected. Flossie was almost as handsome as Lazarus had been, mostly black with tan legs, russet cheeks and eyebrows. The thought of Lazarus saddened him for a moment. Remembering that poor, doomed dog always made him feel that way. He shook his head to clear it and concentrated on making the rounds with Flossie, through the rest of Assisted Living, down the empty connecting hallway and into Skilled Nursing where many folks were confined to bed, and Flossie's visit seemed to mean even more.

Meanwhile, Eden changed into her EverTeen pinafore and white blouse, left books and school clothes in her locker and hurried to the Skilled Nursing wing. She spoke to the nurses and began looking in on residents. "Hi, Miz Barker, anything I can do for you today?" She fluffed up the woman's pillows and helped her find a more comfortable position, then moved on.

On and on, giving what assistance she could until she finally spotted Greg Pendergast pushing the Auxiliary Gift Cart down the hall. *Oh happy day*, she thought. He stopped in front of Mr. King's room, and Eden heard him ask if Mr. K needed anything today. The answer was apparently negative, because Pendergast was back out in the hall in a matter of moments.

Down at the far end of Skilled Nursing, Jimmy Lee watched Eden approach Greg Pendergast and start to talk. Flossie sat at his side, ears erect, her gaze seemingly on Eden too. Jimmy Lee breathed a little prayer that Eden would be all right. She always thought she could take care of herself, but he was feeling uneasy. If Pendergast had actually done something to Miz Cunningham, Eden could be in danger, and Jimmy Lee wanted to be near in case he and Flossie needed to step in.

Eden said something, and Pendergast stepped back. She took a step forward, and Jimmy Lee sucked in a breath. What was she doing? Didn't she know moving like that could make Pendergast feel threatened? Flossie caught Jimmy Lee's mood and stood up. But now Eden was smiling, and Pendergast was nodding his head as if he agreed with whatever she was saying. Jimmy Lee put a calming hand on Flossie's neck and let out the breath he'd been holding. What the heck was going on?

After a while, Eden spotted Jimmy Lee, said a few more words to Pendergast and patted his arm. Then she came down the hall and gave Jimmy Lee her "see-I-told-you-so" look.

"I don't know why you're standing here, Jimmy Lee. You oughta be making the rounds with Flossie. These Skilled Nursing residents are just longing for a visit."

Jimmy Lee couldn't help it, he was just plain mad. How could she risk setting Pendergast off and then put down somebody who cared as much as he did? "Sometimes you don't have a lick of sense," he said, without taking time to think before opening his mouth.

"And sometimes you don't trust me to take care of myself," she answered in the same tone. She gazed up at him and shook her head back and forth. "I was only softening Pendergast up for the kill, just like we planned. Once he thinks we're buddies, I'll find out what we want to know."

Four blocks away, Charlie was running around the track at the municipal park. Late afternoon, when fewer people were there and he could let his mind roam. He needed to think through what Alice had said about everyone having know-how that would help them bring Rodney Cunningham to justice. Well, that was true of George and Willard, a lawyer and an accountant. Maybe even of Fred, who was so suspicious he almost couldn't accept a simple truth when there was one. Yet Fred's suspicions had ended up having something to them after all.

But what did a track coach bring to the team? Nothing much he could see. With his bum knee, he couldn't even run down Rodney, if it ever came to that. All this cogitating was making Charlie feel even worse than when he started running, so he stepped up his pace, trying to wear away those negative thoughts.

He was wheezing around the far turn, when he heard a woman's voice coming up behind. "Hi, Mr. Coleman, remember me? Janice Cunningham, Rodney's wife. We met at the Rotary picnic last summer?"

He stopped and turned. There she was, dressed in powder-blue velour this time with sports bra and running shoes to match.

He was so winded he could barely get a word out, "Of course, Miz Cunningham. How're you today?" Pretty lame, but that's all he could manage.

She gave him a smile that almost blinded, her teeth were so white. Charlie wondered if Fred had done that bleach job. Must've made a tidy little sum, if he did. Then the thought grabbed him that this was the wife of the man they suspected of contributing to Suzie's death. If he didn't downright kill her. That left him dumbstruck.

Janice Cunningham seemed to sense his distress. "I've got a couple bottles of water stashed in my car. I'm dying of thirst. Can I offer you one too?"

Charlie contrived to nod and say, "Most kind." Next thing he knew, she'd cozied up to his arm and was escorting him to a champagne-colored Lexus parked right by the track. She opened the trunk, fished out two one-liter bottles of water, opened them both despite her long, powder-blue nails, and passed one to Charlie.

He watched her full lips surround the top of her bottle and tried to keep his mind on what a Silver Fox might gain from this chance meeting. "I've seen you here before. Rodney doesn't run?"

Her face gave a pretty pout. "He uses the gym out at the Country Club. But I like to run. Just clears everything out — cobwebs, worries, aches and pains."

Charlie said, "Now Miz Cunningham, what would worry a pretty woman like you?" He asked himself if he was laying it on a little thick.

She clearly made an effort to smile and keep it light. "Oh, we all have our worries, don't we?" When she took a final swig from the bottle, upending it, the powder-blue sleeve of her tracksuit fell back, and Charlie saw the deeper blue of a bruise above her wrist.

He must have been staring, because she pulled the sleeve down to her diamond-encrusted watch and said, "Oh my, look what time it is." Her right eye seemed to offer the barest wink as she said, "So nice talking with you that I forgot all about picking up my little Yorkie from the groomer."

She jumped in the car and drove away with a flutter of her fingers. Charlie stood watching with a half-drunk bottle of water and the realization of what he'd seen. The bruise was in the shape of four very large fingers wrapped around her forearm.

ALICE SAT IN EVERGREEN'S CAFE, waiting for George to show up for their nine o'clock meeting. She took a sip of her coffee and surveyed the room. It was as good a place as any to get together. The Cafe offered cold and hot drinks plus snacks from nine in the morning until nine at night. Still early, so very few residents had come in for their mid-morning goodies. That meant not many to see or hear. On the other hand, they'd be meeting in a public place. The last thing Alice needed was someone misinterpreting why George would be leaving her apartment in the morning. Tongues already wagged enough about who was sleeping with whom at Evergreen.

A figure passed the Cafe entrance. Alice glanced at the movement, but it wasn't George, only the florist delivery man heading toward the Independent Living apartments with a vase of flowers in one hand and a potted plant in the other. Beyond him, the window framed blue sky, a blessing after all the rain they'd had, but it seemed blustery too, the trees waving this way and that.

George entered, looking as natty as ever in gray corduroy slacks, gray cashmere V-neck and a blue gingham shirt. Plus his trademark saddle shoes, this time a rather subdued black-on-black. While he got a cup of coffee, Alice glanced down at her own attire — long, heavy cotton skirt in an ethnic print of black and magenta, black wool tunic to mid-thigh and another ethnic print in the soft scarf draped around her neck. You'd be hard-pressed to find two more different tastes in clothes, she reflected.

When George arrived at the table, he was carrying two doughnuts on the tray as well as his coffee. He smiled and passed her one of the doughnuts. "Thought maybe we both could use a little fortifying."

Alice nodded her thanks and noted he'd picked her favorite, a cruller dipped in chocolate. "How'd your meeting go with Farnsworth yesterday?" she said. No need to beat around the bush with George, thank God.

Yet he did raise his eyebrows for a moment, like he was disconcerted to sail immediately into the reason for their meeting. "Very interesting. Sam said he hadn't mentioned it before, because this highway project isn't a done deal. But it sure looks like it's going to happen. Quite a bit of money under the table, some of it rumored to be Rodney's."

"So how would Rodney make money off Suzie's land?" Alice asked. "Would the highway go through it?"

George took a quick sip of his coffee. "Nope, and that'd be a good thing for him. If he got control of Suzie's land, and the highway were built on it, that would be by right of eminent domain, and he wouldn't make much, if anything. No, the corridor is slated to have an exit near Great Oaks, so he'd want to develop it."

"Develop it how?"

George shrugged. "Depends. Couple of hotels, one upscale, one more modest. Some gas stations. Another shopping center. Golf course with houses all around. Use the mansion as a club house.

Lots of possibilities. Rodney's always been clever about property development. He'd know what to do."

"But he doesn't have control of Suzie's land. Her daughters do." Alice took a bite of her cruller, and chocolate icing fell on her lap. She brushed it away and continued. "They'd never let Rodney ruin Great Oaks like that."

"Hard to tell," George said. "Remember Penelope talking about Rodney offering to buy the land and let the girls settle with each other about the house? Wonder what they're thinking about that now?"

Alice grinned. "Time for another memorial bridge game, this time with Brenda sitting in her mother's place."

Over in the lobby between Skilled Nursing and Assisted Living, Trudy noticed Bethanne looking through the glass doors and followed her gaze. Alejandro was exiting the back of the florist van with a couple potted plants. Bethanne hurried to the double doors and opened one for him. A strong wind seemed to blow him into the lobby.

"Hi, Alejandro," Bethanne said with a big smile, "How many today?"

He didn't smile back. "These two and four more. Busy day for Blossoms Aplenty."

"Let me help you then," Bethanne said. "When you come back, we'll carry them together."

That was a surprise to Trudy. The adult Volunteers usually helped deliver flowers when Alejandro had too many for one trip. What was going on? Was Bethanne planning to corner Alejandro about what he'd said to his sister? And then what? Would Alejandro get fired? So unfair. Alejandro was hard-working and kind, and everyone was fond of him. What could she do to save such a special man?

Alejandro nodded and gave Bethanne a weak smile as he hustled past. "The other four are for Assisted Living," he said and glanced at Trudy. It seemed like a cry for help.

"No problem. I'll wait for you," Bethanne said and stationed herself at the Information Desk, right in front of the glass doors and between the two wings.

That blocked Trudy from getting out and made it easy for Bethanne to follow Alejandro when he returned. Sure enough, Alejandro came back, and Bethanne accompanied him out to the van. Trudy walked to the glass doors and held one ajar as if to help. The gusting wind made it hard to keep the door open, but she wanted to watch and listen.

Alejandro leaned inside the van and handed Bethanne two pots with ribbons, a magenta geranium and a bronze mum. Then he picked up a turtle-shaped pot of mixed succulents and an orange sphere with different kinds of green leaves. The wind threatened to ruin the ribbons, if not the plants, and both people turned their backs to shield the pots from the gusts.

"You and me, Alejandro," Bethanne said. "No wind'll blow us away."

Trudy leaned against the door with all her weight to keep it open. Bethanne nodded her thanks as they passed. Trudy didn't bother to look up room numbers. Bethanne knew where every resident's bed was. The Volunteer Coordinator led the way to the door closest to the lobby. "Hi, Miz Brown," she said, "Alejandro's got something for you."

Trudy didn't know what to do. She was the only one at the Information Desk, so she couldn't leave her post. But Alejandro might need her help. She could hear Mrs. Brown rising to the occasion, oo-ing and ah-ing over the succulents, saying they were her favorite and wasn't her nephew nice to remember.

Trudy leaned out to watch Bethanne moving on to the next two recipients and handing over her pots of flowers. That left the resident at the end of the hall, and it seemed to Trudy that Bethanne had planned it that way.

By the grace of God, Greg Pendergast appeared with the Gift Cart, and Trudy could ask a favor. "I'm so sorry to bother you, but I need to go to the ladies' room," she said, trying to look embarrassed. "Could you possibly cover the Information Desk for a few minutes?"

"My pleasure," he said as if he understood her problem, and Trudy took off down the Assisted Living hallway as fast as her painful joints would allow. As always, she was a little creaky for the first few steps, but then her joints limbered up, and she could move pretty well. The ladies' room was just opposite the door of the last flower recipient. Ahead, she saw Bethanne open the resident's door so Alejandro could go in.

When Trudy got to the ladies' room, Bethanne was paying attention to what was happening in the room across the hall. Trudy paused to watch and listen. She could see past Bethanne to Mr. Dent napping in his recliner. The sound of Alejandro's steps woke him, and the old man's wrinkles lifted into a smile. "Now what do we have here?" he said.

Alejandro put down the pot on the table next to the recliner. "Beautiful plants from someone who loves you."

Mr. Dent took Alejandro's smooth, brown hand between his two veined and liver-spotted ones. "You've made my day, young man." He reached into his pocket. "Let me give you a tip." He brought out a quarter and placed it in Alejandro's palm. "I know it's not much, but it's what I have."

Alejandro started to refuse but then seemed to think better of it. "Thank you, Mr. Dent. You've made my day too."

Trudy couldn't pause any longer. She had to get inside the ladies' room or risk looking shifty. She slipped in, leaving the light off and the door open a crack. She could see out, but hopefully they couldn't see in.

Bethanne took Alejandro by the elbow and steered him into the empty third wing. "That was a kind thing you did," she said. "You made Mr. Dent feel like he'd done something good. You have that gift, making old people feel like they amount to something."

Alejandro put his hands in his pockets. "In my country, they do. We look up to our elders and ask them for advice."

"And here we often forget that," Bethanne said. Her words struck Trudy like Bethanne was trying to soften him up. Alejandro nodded, and Bethanne continued, "The last time we were together, you seemed like you were going to tell me something, but then we were interrupted." Trudy thought the Volunteer Coordinator was purposely standing between Alejandro and the Assisted Living wing, so it was awkward for him to get around her.

"Something?" he said.

"Something fishy, something not quite right." Bethanne's smile seemed affected to Trudy. "Please tell me," the Volunteer Coordinator said. "I need your help."

Alejandro looked past her and seemed reassured. Maybe he was checking to see if anyone was near. He sucked in his lips and chewed them. He peeped past Bethanne again. "You won't tell anyone what I say?"

"Not if I can help it. I'll try never to say who told me. How's that?"

He rubbed his hands up and down his lower face and along his jaw. He gaped past her one more time, raised his eyes to heaven and opened his mouth. "I saw a woman leaving Missis Cunningham's room just before the nurses ran in."

Trudy felt her heart jolt as Bethanne said. "What nurses? When?" That was exactly what Trudy wanted to know, and she dared to peek out just a little more.

"The nurses who tried to save Missis Cunningham's life." Alejandro said. "I took off down the hall. I didn't want to get in their way."

Bethanne was obviously holding herself very still and making her voice as gentle as she could. "Who was the woman?"

Alejandro shook his head, his dark eyes sad. "I don't know. I never saw her before, but she sure was in a hurry to get out of there."

9

ALICE AND GEORGE WERE STARTING TO rise from their Cafe chairs when Charlie dashed in and plopped down at their table without asking if they'd mind. He unzipped the jacket of his navy tracksuit, put a foot up on one knee, nodded at George and grinned at Alice.

"I've been looking all over for you," he said to her. Phoned you last night, but no answer."

"I was at the movies," Alice said, feeling a little off-base. What did he want?

"Oh, yeah, *Ben Hur* in the Rec Room. Didn't like that movie the first time around." Charlie said. "Can't stand Charlton Heston trying to act like a jock. Whole thing was trick photography."

"You've been looking for Alice?" George prompted.

"Yeah." Charlie gazed at her. "Went by your apartment this morning, but no one there." He grinned again. "Then I remembered you like to come here for a morning break." He opened his arms wide. "So here I am. Wait 'til you hear what I saw."

In excruciating detail, he told about his chance meeting with Janice Cunningham the day before. How she moved up behind him, maybe coming onto him, what she was wearing, how she put her pouty lips around the bottle's mouth.

About halfway through, George glanced at Alice, and she gave him a wide-eyed shake of the head. She didn't know where this was going either.

Finally, Charlie got to the point. "So what did I see on that bare arm? A big, blue bruise where four fingers had grabbed her so hard, they left their mark." Charlie gave a final grin and settled back. "Had to've been Rodney. Who else is gonna hurt her like that?"

George shifted in his chair like he was uncomfortable. "Could be another man in her life."

Charlie put both hands on the table. "I don't think so. Janice Cunningham knows which side her bread is buttered on. Woman's covered in diamonds — watch, wedding band, engagement ring with a rock that'd choke a horse. Never wears the same tracksuit twice, always expensive with sports bra and shoes to match."

Alice wanted to ask how Charlie knew about the bra but thought better of it. "So you're saying she puts up with abuse from Rodney in order to live the good life."

Charlie nodded. "Let's face it. She's a trophy wife. Used to be Rodney's secretary. Sleeping with him long before the divorce. Probably thought she'd caught the brass ring when he proposed." He winked. "Rumor was he got her pregnant, and she got a ring."

"Suzie divorced Rodney, because he got Janice pregnant?" George said.

"No," Alice answered. "The divorce was way before he married Janice."

Charlie smirked. "Maybe Janice just saw the course was clear and forgot to take her pills." He shrugged. "No baby ever came though. Lots of gossip about that."

George shook his head. "We're getting awfully far from what we know to be true. Let's stick to the facts."

"Okay," Charlie said. "The fact is I saw a four-finger bruise on Janice Cunningham's arm."

George gestured with both palms up. "So maybe Rodney's mistreating his wife. What's that got to do with Suzie's death?"

Alice looked from George to Charlie, who answered. "Proves he's violent. If he's hurting Janice, he'd have hurt Suzie too."

She folded her arms across her chest. "He did hurt her. That was one reason Suzie gave in court for wanting a divorce."

Charlie seemed to mimic Alice's posture without realizing what he was doing."Just a little more proof of how far a man might go. If Rodney habitually hurt his wives, he might kill one too."

Trudy pleaded a headache and left her post at the Information Desk early. She'd never done that before, and she felt guilty. Two sins in one afternoon. First lying to Greg, so she could spy on Bethanne and Alejandro. Maybe that was two sins and lying to get to Alice as soon as possible was the third. She knew she was weak, prey to snooping and even to telling, but this was a bit excessive, even for her. At least she hadn't had to lie to Bethanne, who'd finished her shift and gone home.

She hustled across the manicured gardens of Evergreen, looking a bit bedraggled after all the rain they'd had and now getting tossed by a heavy breeze. Happy to get out of the wind, Trudy scurried down the hallway to Alice's apartment and rang the doorbell. No answer. What if Alice wasn't home?

But she was. Alice opened the door with an apology, "Sorry, I must have dozed off over my book." Her Siamese tried to dart out the door, and both women bent to prevent her escape. Alice scooped up the cat and led the way back inside.

Then it was Trudy's turn to apologize, "I'm sorry too, but this really can't wait. A woman was in Suzie's room just before she died."

"Wow," Alice said and gestured Trudy inside. The grandmother followed Alice to her tiny kitchen, where her friend poured them each a cup of stale coffee from an ancient machine. Then Alice led the way to her dining table and let Trudy tell the whole tale without interrupting. Meanwhile, the cat curled up on Alice's lap and went to sleep.

Once Trudy had finished, Alice spoke. "But Rodney said at the funeral he was there when Suzie died. Said he got down on his knees and prayed with her."

"That's what I was thinking too," Trudy said. "So he was lying? Fred's right?"

"Or Rodney arrived after the woman. Who could she be?"

"One of Suzie's daughters going for help?" Trudy asked.

"Doesn't make sense. A daughter would've stuck around, waiting for news. This woman was in a hurry to leave." Alice paused. "Unless she had something to hide."

Trudy pushed up her slipping spectacles. "I was wondering the same thing. Makes me feel bad just to imagine it. One of Suzie's daughters...?" She shuddered. "I can't even bear to say it."

Alice folded her arms on the table. "Okay, let's not rush to conclusions. Who else would be visiting? A friend? Someone from Evergreen?"

Trudy nodded. "Could be. I didn't think of that. But if it was a friend, why would she rush get away?"

THE SILVER FOXES 73

"You said Alejandro didn't want to get in the way of the nurses. Maybe the friend felt the same."

"Maybe," Trudy said. "But who would it be? Why hasn't she said anything?" Then a thought shocked her like she'd touched a frayed electrical wire. "Could it be Anne-Marie? They were good friends." Trudy lowered her head and wagged it back and forth. "It's just too awful to contemplate."

Alice reached across the table and patted her hand. "But we have to face up to it. Now that memorial bridge game with Brenda is more important than ever."

Trudy nodded, too sick to reply.

Over in Skilled Nursing, the Volunteers were all going off-duty and heading home. Eden caught up with Greg Pendergast as he was wheeling the Gift Cart down the hall. He wasn't much taller than she was, maybe five-seven or so. It was easy to look him in the face and smile.

"Hi, Mr. Pendergast," she said. "Sell much today?"

He smiled back. "Enough. Seems like magazines do best. Folks laid up in bed want to read something light."

She turned her upper body slightly toward him as they walked along. Easier to see his reactions that way, though she could have done without seeing the dandruff nestled among the folds of his gray Evergreen tabard.

"Seems that way to me too," she said. "Even when I read to them, they just want to be entertained."

Eden paused in the hallway to let someone pass, and Pendergast waited with her. She did her best to appear ashamed. "Guess you know I'm the one who told Bethanne you were reading to the residents."

His nod seemed a little stiff, and she continued. "I feel bad about that. I finally realized you were reading only to Miz Suzie. You two must've been special friends, and I was jumping to wild conclusions."

He started pushing the cart again, his rubber soles squeaking on the linoleum as he headed toward the storage closet at a good clip. Eden kept pace. "I'm awfully sorry, Mr. Pendergast."

He stopped and looked her in the eye. His voice seemed as squeaky as his shoes, and his mouth turned down. "I'm sure you are. Never a good thing to rush to conclusions." He pressed on to the cart's closet, and Eden passed by with a tingle of excitement. He'd as much as admitted that he was visiting Miz Suzie on a regular basis. Now what did that mean?

She entered the Volunteer locker room hugging herself. Still more to this story, for sure.

10

A COUPLE DAYS BEFORE THE SECOND memorial bridge game, the Silver Foxes met at Alice's apartment to share information and make sure they all were on the same page.

She asked George to lead off first. He reported on what his friend, the lawyer Farnsworth, had said about the plan for the new highway to include an exit near Great Oaks.

Willard spoke up."Remember that song from *Cabaret*?" He sang the opening phrase in a surprisingly good baritone, "Money, money, money, money, money... " ending with, "Told you." He leaned back with arms crossed and a smile that approached a sneer.

Charlie told about seeing the bruise on Janice Cunningham's arm. Of course, he had to give all the details, and of course, Fred had put his two cents in. "Dirty old man. What were you looking at her bra for?" Charlie blushed and glanced at Trudy. Alice was relieved to see her concentrate on her own report and pay no attention to Fred's barb.

Trudy kept her account of overhearing Alejandro short. She and Alice had previously agreed there was no point in telling how she happened to hear. She focused on Alejandro seeing a woman bolt out of Suzie's room just before she died. While Trudy was reporting, Alice kept an eye on Anne-Marie, but if she had been the one rushing away, she certainly didn't show it. Not a muscle moved, not even the tiny ones around eyes or mouth.

In the end, the Silver Foxes agreed on a strategy, not only for the bridge game but also next steps afterwards.

Now, prepping just before that event, Alice was putting finishing touches to the Game Room and praying everything would go according to plan. Brenda was famous for her hostess skills, so Alice was nervous, trying to make everything right. She'd never been famous for her own hostess skills, preferring practicality over folderol. Yet here she was, fluffing up a vase of mauve spider mums and laying out pretty bridge tallies she'd ordered online with coasters to match. *Ugh*, she thought, *this isn't you* and vowed never to get sucked into this kind of nonsense again.

She glanced out the window. The day had turned cloudy and gray. That gave her more worries. Would Brenda drop out at the last minute because of threatening skies?

A fuss sounded at the door, and Anne-Marie entered with Brenda, both of them giving the once-over to Alice's preparations. They were followed close behind by the rest of the Silver Foxes. Trudy immediately remarked, "Oh, how lovely. Everything in fall colors. You've really outdone yourself, Alice."

"So nice of you to come," Alice said to Brenda, taking her hand in what she hoped was a warm clasp.

Alice was tall and gawky, while Brenda was taller and willowy. Suzie's daughter glanced down from her five-feet-ten and said, "Well, I might have been first invited, since I was first-born."

That left an awkward pause, but Trudy, as usual, saved the day. "Best for last." She smiled. "Besides, we knew you were always busy, while Penelope has more time on her hands."

Brenda took off her camel-hair coat and tossed it on the couch, along with her designer umbrella. She put fingertips to her cashmere and pearls, seeming a bit mollified. "Where do I sit?"

George held out a chair. "Opposite me. I'm your partner today." He looked particularly debonair, dressed in gray flannels and a black turtleneck. *Whatever does the trick*, Alice thought.

Trudy smiled up at Alice with a wink and helped get everyone else to their seats. Alice moved Brenda's coat and umbrella to the closet while Trudy poured ice water into the crystal glasses she'd donated to the cause.

Brenda played like a demon, slapping down cards and snatching tricks. Thank God she was playing with George, Alice thought. Who knew what would have happened if Brenda had got Charlie. But that couldn't have happened, because she and George had thought this through very carefully. They wanted Brenda happy and ready to talk.

Still, it was uphill a lot of the way, with Brenda showing her condescension at how others played. All the Silver Foxes knew the agenda was to get Brenda to bring them up-to-date on Rodney's plans, but only Trudy and Alice had another goal too. They needed to learn if Brenda was the woman Alejandro saw darting from Suzie's room right before she died. They were still questioning whether Anne-Marie could be a suspect, but they had no idea how to check up on that.

Alice was concerned that Brenda's patronizing style might set off the more volatile players and ruin the strategy so carefully planned with George and Trudy. Happily, Anne-Marie was sitting at the same table, partnered with Fred, both of them decent enough players yet weak enough to make Brenda feel superior. Besides, Anne-Marie was still sucking up, and Brenda liked that. So maybe everything would go all right.

Finally the bridge play ended, all the points were tallied, and Brenda and George came out on top. Alice breathed a sigh of relief and gestured to the buffet which the Evergreen staff had organized only moments before the game ended. Everyone moved to the chintz couches and chairs. Alice served the petits fours to Brenda first, while George poured her coffee and passed the cream and sugar. Alice wondered if they were overdoing it, but Brenda seemed to be relishing the attention.

Anne-Marie took off with gusto. "Tell us what's happening with Great Oaks. I'm just dying to hear what you-all have decided."

Brenda rested her coffee cup in its saucer and grimaced. "I'm determined to have the house. Penelope and her school-teacher husband are nowhere near being able to keep it up. Let alone afford the renovations. If they've got any sense, they'll put whatever they get from Dad into a college fund for their kids."

Alice was concerned the rest of the Foxes might jump in, but they seemed fascinated by the conversation so far.

Anne-Marie wrinkled her brow. "Is it terribly run down?"

"Just shocking," Brenda replied. "Momma let the whole place go after the divorce. It's going to cost us a fortune." She patted her dark brown bob. "But we can afford it."

Alice reflected that with a surgeon for husband, there was no doubt of that. Everyone knew they made tons of money. Fred snorted, and Alice rushed in to head him off. "So no B&B, like Penelope wants?"

Brenda took a bite of her petit four and put the rest down like she'd tasted something disappointing. "Can you imagine? Strangers sleeping in our ancestral home and grubby children running around a petting farm? That's what Penelope has in mind, but it's not going to happen."

George smiled at Brenda like she was an astute legal associate who'd just found the best precedent ever. "So your father will buy the land, and you'll buy out Penelope?"

Willard was nodding, and Alice hoped he could hold off saying what he was no doubt thinking about the money.

Brenda pulled in an audible breath and raised her eyebrows. "Well, it's not settled yet, but that's the way it'll go. Dad can have most of the land. Bill and I will take five acres around the house, so we'll be protected no matter what happens."

George gave a slight nod. "What's going to happen to the rest?"

Brenda started to answer, but Anne-Marie put in her two cents. "I can hardly wait to see what you do with the old place."

Alice gritted her teeth. They needed to hear the answer to George's question, but Anne-Marie had steered them into a detour. Why would she do that? She'd been there for the strategy discussion. Was she helping Brenda cover up?

Brenda was answering. "I've already hired a decorator to re-design the interiors and a contractor to draw up renovation plans." Her smile failed to move all her face. "With estimates for now. We'll be ready to go when the time comes."

"Sounds like you've just about got it wrapped up," Charlie said, looking around the group with a grin.

Fred started to say something, but Brenda pointedly looked at Anne-Marie. "You must come visit when it's all finished.

"I'd love to," Anne-Marie said.

Brenda stood up, a clear signal she was ready to go. Alice nodded at Trudy, who immediately suggested to Anne-Marie that she supervise the Evergreen staff in clearing up. Anne-Marie liked few things more than being in charge, and once she took over, Alice and Trudy were free to walk Brenda out to her car. George was waylaying Brenda, helping her put on her camel-hair coat, complimenting her on her play and awarding her the kind of smile he used to bestow on the jury.

Trudy took Brenda's arm and started out the door with Alice close behind, carrying her umbrella. "Lovely to have you with us this afternoon," Trudy said to Brenda. "I've seen you and Bill at church but always too far away to speak." She favored Brenda with her most grandmotherly look and continued, "You must be missing your mother so much."

Brenda seemed to be trying to draw away, but Trudy held on like she needed the physical support.

"What?" Brenda said. "Oh yes, we all do."

As they arrived at Brenda's dark green Mercedes, Trudy said, "Were you able to be with her at the end?"

"What?" Brenda repeated.

Like a parrot, Alice thought. Suzie's daughter was off-kilter. Definitely the right decision to let Trudy tackle her. Who'd suspect a kindly grandmother of conducting an interrogation?

Brenda glanced up at the overcast sky and grabbed her umbrella from Alice's hand. She put fingertips on the door handle, and the car automatically unlocked. Brenda thrust the door open, smoothed her coat under her slender thighs and slipped into the driver's seat. "Oh, no, no, no. I was playing golf out at the Country Club. I have a standing reservation with friends for every Tuesday. Momma was gone by the time I got there." She hit the ignition button like it was a target and drove off without a goodbye.

Alice smiled down at Trudy. "Easy enough to check that."

11

THAT EVENING, ALICE WAS WATCHING the local news before bed
when the screen shifted from the studio to a country road lit by bright
lights on tall stands. In the background, a tow truck was trying to pull
a vehicle up an embankment, and an ambulance crew was bundling
a body for transport.

The field reporter was saying, "A man identified as Alejandro
Garcia apparently fell asleep and drove over the embankment behind
me. Mr. Garcia was well-known in Lewiston as the delivery man
for Blossoms Aplenty, a man who was always ready with a smile as
beautiful as the flowers he carried..."

With the reporter's first sentence, Alice's heart started
thumping like it would leap out of her chest. She didn't hear his
third sentence, because her phone began to ring, first with one Silver
Fox, then another, all asking if she'd heard the news and what were
they to think. No one would be able to get to sleep now, so she invited
everybody over, put away the cat and started the coffee pot. Trudy
said she'd bring some home-made cookies her daughter had dropped
off the day before.

The Silver Foxes trickled in, one-by-one, most already in their
nightclothes with robe and slippers. Only Anne-Marie was fully

dressed and coiffed, her make up clearly fresh. George came last, still in what he'd worn to the bridge game, but looking uncharacteristically disheveled. His black turtleneck seemed to sag.

He accepted a cup, helped himself to a sugar cookie and said, "Apologies for being tardy. I wanted to talk with one of the Sheriff's men first and see if there were anything more to learn. He's been a source before when I needed information." George crossed his legs and shook his head, his mouth in a straight line. "Turns out there is more, and we're going to be suspicious."

The whole group leaned in as he continued. "This won't be out until tomorrow's press conference, but there was a homeless man sleeping in the woods. He had a tarp strung over a line between two trees, a dark tarp, so he wasn't likely to be spotted, but open at the ends, so he saw what happened."

Alice felt like she wanted to climb inside George's brain and learn the whole story without having to wait for him to tell it. She took a sip of coffee, but it just made her jitters worse.

Charlie interrupted the flow of George's story. "Was that the first night he was up there?"

"Don't know," George said. "I didn't ask that. What I do know is that he ran down to help and found Alejandro's phone thrown from the wreck. It was still working, so the man called 9-1-1. When Sheriff Price arrived, the guy reported that he heard the screech of tires, so he looked out of his shelter. He saw a dark SUV come over the line and force Alejandro off the road. He didn't hear a bang, so there probably wasn't a collision."

Gasps filled the room, and Alice clutched her hands to her chest as George continued. "This is all on the Q.T., every word of it. We can't say anything to anybody until the press conference." He gave a grim smile. "Alejandro's car is too banged up to tell if it were hit or not. The tracks are inconclusive, and it was too dark for the guy to see if it was a man or a woman."

Fred grinned in triumph. "Rodney has a dark SUV."

Willard sneered. "So does just about every family around here. Even Brenda's got a Mercedes SUV, dark green."

"Could have been anybody," Anne-Marie said. "Or nobody. George said the tracks are inconclusive."

"I think it's pretty clear *somebody* drove Alejandro off the road," Alice said. "What we don't know is who."

The Silver Foxes hashed and rehashed all the information about Alejandro's death without coming to any conclusions. But they did work out who would do what next. They went to their beds well after midnight. Trudy tossed and turned but couldn't get to sleep. Probably no one else could, either.

Trudy searched her conscience. Was she to blame for Alejandro's death by telling the Silver Foxes about what he saw? Anne-Marie had heard, of course. If she was the woman he saw hurrying away from Suzie's room, could Anne-Marie have driven him off the road? Did Anne-Marie still have Tom's old SUV stored somewhere? Trudy shuddered. *Please God, don't let it be my fault, the sin of an old woman who listens in dark closets and speaks before she gets her brain working.*

Whether that was true or not, what could, what should she do now? Everybody seemed to have a task but her. George was going to stay in touch with the Sheriff's Deputy in case there was more news. Willard and Fred were planning to play a round of golf at the Country Club and try to discover if Brenda had really been there the day of her mother's death. Charlie was aiming to find out whether Rodney's trophy wife had ever visited Suzie while she was in Skilled Nursing. Although it hadn't been discussed with the group for obvious reasons, Alice was going to take Anne-Marie to lunch and find a way to ask if she'd been with Suzie just before the nurses rushed in to help. She could probably ask about Tom's SUV too.

That left Trudy with nothing to contribute. Of course, everyone said she'd brought in a major clue with the information that Alejandro had seen a woman leaving Suzie's room just before the nurses rushed in. They were trying to make her feel better. But she didn't feel better. Alejandro was dead, and maybe it was her fault. There must be something she could do to make things right, if only she could think what.

Bethanne sat at her weekly lunch with Mae and an appetite that had totally decamped. It was the day after Alejandro's crash, and she felt sick to her stomach. She and Mae were in the back booth, so they could talk, but now Bethanne was having trouble knowing how to start.

Mae glanced up from her meatloaf. "Don't try to hold it in. I know something's bothering you. Get it out, and let's talk it over."

Bethanne scanned the area to make sure nobody was near. The booth behind them was empty, and the closest table was full of men all talking at once about football. "I feel guilty," she said. "Did you see the press conference this morning?"

Mae wiped her mouth with a paper napkin and smiled. "'Fraid not. Too busy diapering my granddaughter. Lord, I thought I was done with that once I raised my own kids. But young folks nowadays need all the help they can get, working two jobs just to make ends meet." She put her super-sized hand over the top of Bethanne's slender one. "What's happened to make you feel guilty?"

Bethanne's throat seemed to close, and she had to swallow to get it working again. "Alejandro's dead."

"The flower man you were telling me about? The one who wanted to talk with you? What happened?"

"Somebody ran him off the road. Driving a dark SUV."

"Oh, dear Lord. They don't know who?"

"No." Bethanne felt tears pricking her eyes. "Alejandro finally told me what was bothering him, but I never told anybody. Now he's dead, and I don't know what to do."

"So tell me now."

Bethanne blinked back her heartache and related what Alejandro had said about a woman rushing out of Suzie Cunningham's room right before the nurses responded to a Code Blue. "But I didn't do anything," she said. "I was worried maybe he was an illegal alien, and I didn't want to get him in trouble. Besides, Miz Cunningham's death was ruled natural causes."

Mae's eyes got big. "And her husband cremated her just as fast as he could. Even though the family's old-time Baptist."

The two friends sat looking at each other for a while, considering what Mae had said.

"That woman could've been anybody," Bethanne said. "Alejandro could've made a mistake about what he saw. Besides, at the funeral, Rodney Cunningham said he was there when his wife died." She paused and frowned. "Am I just trying to make myself feel better? What should I do?"

Mae reached across the table and gave Bethanne's arm a

reassuring pat. "Maybe talk with Alejandro's sister, find out if she knows anything. Check the body shops to see if anyone brought in a dark SUV for repairs to a fender. Do we know if the SUV crashed into Alejandro's car?"

Bethanne nodded, lost in thought. Finally, she spoke. "No, we don't know if there was contact or not, but I can definitely find a way to talk with his sister. How many body shops are there in Lewiston?"

Mae sighed. "Enough. Even more if you check the whole county. I'd volunteer to help, but no mechanic is going to answer a black woman asking about a car belonging to the richest white man in town."

Bethanne shook her head. "I can't imagine them talking to me either. What excuse would I give for wanting to know?" She took in a deep breath and blew it out through her nose. "Okay, let's concentrate on the sister first and deal with the SUV later."

Charlie put his part of the Silver Foxes' plan into action the same day Bethanne and Mae were meeting over lunch. He got to the track early in the afternoon and hung around until he saw Janice Cunningham drive into the parking lot. He started running in a middle lane, hoping she'd catch up and speak to him. It was sunny and dry, so there were lots more people than usual. He was concerned she wouldn't see him. Sometimes, it felt like he was in a crowd, but he ran on and kept an eye out for her. Today, she had on a red tracksuit, so that made it easier. He varied his pace, changing lanes so he could fake a chance meeting.

Finally he got directly in front of her and stumbled. She couldn't help but reach out and grab his arm to keep him on his feet. The frown of concern under her wispy bangs seemed genuine. "Mr. Coleman! Are you okay? Did you hurt your ankle?"

What a great idea, he thought and put it to work. "Not sure. Maybe a little. Could you help me over to a bench?"

She held his elbow, steadying him. Charlie limped just enough to be convincing but not so badly that he couldn't follow through with his plan.

"Thanks," he said when they sat down side by side. "Stubbed my toe on something." He rotated his ankle back and forth. "Seems okay. Nothing broken."

"Does it hurt?"

"Some. I'll be fine."

He kept rotating his ankle in line with her knees, so it was awkward for her to get up and leave. All the while encouraging her to chat about what she'd been doing since he'd last seen her. Mostly shopping, it appeared, but she seemed starved to talk about it. Maybe Rodney wasn't paying her enough attention?

Finally the time was right to make his next move. He reached down and rubbed his ankle. "I'm afraid I ran over here, as usual. Any chance you could give me a lift back to Evergreen?"

She hesitated, and he said, "Do you know where it is? Been there before?"

Janice shook her head so hard, her blond-streaked hair flew out to the sides. "Are you kidding? Rodney's first wife lived there. No way I'd want to even get near." She smiled at Charlie, "But she's gone now, so I can drive you over. Come on."

She helped lift him to his feet, and Charlie almost forgot to limp. She'd never been to Evergreen. Was that the truth?

12

WHILE CHARLIE WAS GETTING A LIFT home, Trudy was still wallowing in melancholy. She recognized she was feeling sorry for herself, which made her more disappointed, so the cycle went round and round. She should have got out and walked right after breakfast. Her doctor encouraged her to do that everyday to loosen polymyalgia rheumatica's stiff and painful joints. But today she'd been too demoralized to go out. The result was PMR symptoms hanging on longer than usual.

She knew walking lifted her spirits too. She needed to get busy and stop thinking so much about herself, her problems and her guilt. She pushed her body up from her chair, put on her Nikes and just did it. Once she was outside, it didn't take many steps in the fall sunshine to confirm that she was doing what she should have done hours ago. Exercise always helped her body and mind, but sometimes she got lazy and indulged her problems instead of doing something about them.

The Evergreen campus had been carefully planted and tended over the years. All the buff brick buildings were one-story, built around courtyards with trees, grass and seasonal flowers so something was always blooming. Walkways led through buildings and courtyards, so it was easy to go all over campus. She rambled here and there as the mood struck her.

Trudy walked into the lobby of the facility that housed Skilled Nursing and Assisted Living, waved at the Volunteers and went on out to the building's courtyard. That garden was particularly attractive this time of year, and she was looking forward to sitting on a bench and enjoying the fall colors. But two people were already there. And a dog. Now what?

Then she heard the voices. Eden first, because Trudy realized that's who was on the bench, Eden with her young man and Flossie. The grandmother heard Eden say "Miz Suzie," and she had to listen. Snooping or not, this could be important.

"I think Pendergast was having an affair with Miz Suzie," Eden was saying, "and now that she's gone, he's back to behaving like a normal Volunteer."

"You can't know that," Jimmy Lee said. "Maybe he liked her, but you don't know they was having an affair. Besides, she was at least ten years older'n him."

"So? You prejudiced against older women? All I know is, Miz Suzie sure perked up every time he visited. Just full of the joy of it."

Like Charlie, Willard and Fred also had a goal for the day after the Silver Foxes saw what happened to Alejandro on TV. They started off playing golf at the Country Club, bickering like they always did. For the retired accountant and dentist, it was a sign of their long-standing affection for one another.

"That's a gimme," Willard said when his putt rolled two feet from the hole.

"When elephants fly," Fred responded, but it was too late. Willard had picked up his ball and started toward the tee for the next hole. "You better try the ladies' tee if we wanna get home tonight," Fred called after him.

Willard hooked his drive into the rough. Fred grinned and said, "Maybe you should take up knitting with Trudy."

Once they were on the green, Fred had to view his putt from all angles. Several times. Willard couldn't stand it. This was exactly how Fred played bridge. "Playing golf with you is like watching grass grow," the retired accountant said. "Hit the damn ball, and let's see if we can't finish before the Pro Shop closes."

And so it went all afternoon, until they finished the eighteenth hole nearly even, as usual. Willard handed over a couple of bills, "Here's the two bucks I owe you for the point spread."

Fred snatched them from his hand. "Sure feels good to take you to the cleaners."

"That's not the cleaners," Willard said. "I beat you by three last time."

"Bullshit."

"Now, now," Willard said, "Golf is a gentleman's game."

"Then maybe you should ask for your money back."

Willard headed for the golf cart. "Come on, let's find out whether Brenda was here the day her mother died."

"I'm driving."

"No, I'm driving. You nearly put us in the ditch on the fifteenth."

Fred's small and wiry body made it easy to take advantage of Willard's bulk. The former dentist tossed his clubs in the back of the cart and got in the driver's seat. Willard heaved his bag in and lumbered to sit beside his friend.

"Pro Shop, here we come!" Fred shouted and gunned it, Willard hanging on like he'd fly out on the curves.

They turned in the cart and headed for the reservation desk. "Hi," Fred said to the college kid who worked part-time, "we need to check if a friend of ours played some weeks ago. He said he was in a foursome with Brenda Milford? She was the one made the reservation."

"What's the date?" the kid asked, and both men were stumped. They'd failed to bring that critical information.

"Here," said Willard, "let me look at my calendar." He quickly thumbed his cell phone and found the date of Suzie's funeral. Then he backtracked from there. "Looks like it was September second or thereabouts. Can you check a couple dates either side of that?"

Fred wagged his head and smirked. "We got a bet about who played when. Bottle of scotch involved."

The kid smiled and kept scrolling through the reservations list. "I don't see Miz Milford's name anywhere in September *or* August. Are you sure she made the reservation?"

"That's what she said," Willard answered, and Fred's eyes smiled as he looked up at his friend.

Alice opened her door to Trudy's insistent knocking. "I know all I seem to do is bother you," the grandmother said, "and I know I'm so snoopy I'm ashamed. But I just overheard another clue to Suzie's death."

Trudy was shaking with emotion. Alice put an arm around her shoulders, brought her inside and made them both a cup of tea. With toast and honey, just like her own grandmother used to do when Alice showed up at her door, upset over nasty taunts from classmates about a girl liking math and science. Alice let Trudy talk until she got it all out, not only what she'd overheard but also how she felt about spying on others' conversations. Thankfully, Chow-Fan slept through the whole thing, curled up on one of the beige chairs.

"Were you afraid Eden and Jimmy Lee would see you? Or his dog sense you were there?" Alice asked.

Trudy shrugged. "You know how it is with young people. I probably could've walked right by the two of them, and they'd never have noticed. Old people are invisible." She paused to give a lop-sided smile. "I'm an old country girl. The wind was blowing the wrong way for Flossie to know I was there."

Alice could feel there was more to it. "Is something else bothering you?"

Trudy seemed to be trying to hold something in, like she didn't want to trouble Alice more. Finally, she talked about her guilt over what happened to Alejandro.

"I understand how you feel," Alice said. "I've already asked Anne-Marie to lunch next week. We've both got our doubts about her really being a suspect. Hopefully, we can put that worry to bed right after I talk with her."

"You going to ask her about Tom's SUV?" Trudy asked.

Alice nodded. "Yes, I thought of that too. Let's find out if she has access to what could have been the murder-car."

Alice felt guilty herself. She'd finagled everyone into investigating Suzie's death without thinking through what that might require them to do. Now Trudy, surely one of God's own Christian women, felt sinful. And whose fault was that?

"Should we stop trying to find out what happened?" she asked Trudy.

Her guest was no longer shaking with emotion, but she took a long time to answer, like she was searching her conscience or maybe praying. "No," she said. "I don't like how nosy I am, that I like to snoop into other folks' affairs. It's always been my cross to bear, ever since I was a girl. Even worse is everything we're learning. Suzie probably didn't die from natural causes." Trudy's face was the saddest Alice had ever seen, as she continued "And if that's what happened, what kind of sinner would I be to look the other way?"

"So what do you want to do?" Alice asked.

This time, Trudy's smile was jubilant. "Two things. I'm going to talk with Alejandro's sister. And I want you to come to church with me."

Now it was Alice's turn to feel downcast. "You know I'm not a church-goer."

"Yes, I know. But this time, you'll want to. Suzie went to my church. So does Greg Pendergast. His wife has early-onset Alzheimers, so he comes alone, and I remember him sitting with Suzie more than once. Made it seem like it just happened, but now I'm wondering. Come with me this Sunday, and we can *just happen* to sit with him and talk afterwards at the social."

George drove to the Sheriff's office the next afternoon, looking for Ben Kishbaugh, the deputy who was usually good for some inside information. To George's surprise, he was ushered in to see Jerry Price.

Years of trial work had honed George's innate ability to think fast on his feet. He sat in one of the scuffed wooden chairs, crossed his long legs and smiled. "In the neighborhood and thought I'd stop by to see if you can say anything about Alejandro Garcia's death."

He raised his shoulders and shook his head. "Don't mean to pry, and I know you can't reveal everything in a pending case. But you can imagine how all the Evergreen residents are feeling about losing such a kind young man. His death really left a hole." He paused. "I suppose you've already checked the body shops about a dark SUV needing a fender repaired?"

Sheriff Price lit a cigar. "Sure did, but that's privileged information in an on-going investigation." He grinned. "Don't bullshit a bullshitter, George. You may not be practicing law anymore, but you've got a bigger motive than you say for wanting to know what happened." He leaned back in his desk chair, forcing the spring as far as it would go. "Otherwise, you wouldn't have called one of my deputies the night of the accident."

George lost his poker face, and the Sheriff picked up on it. "Oh yeah," Price said, "I've known for years about that little deal you have with Ben. Suits me to leak info when I need to." He wagged his head back and forth. "But you're retired now. What's got you so interested in this case?"

The two men stared at each other for a while, neither of them speaking. George thought about what he should tell and how much detail he should give. He wasn't in this alone. He had to consider the Silver Foxes. Finally, he reversed the crossing of his legs and said, "I've got some reason to believe that Garcia's death may be connected to another suspicious one."

The Sheriff sat up with a bang as his chair sprung forward. "What death? I don't know of any other suspicious death."

"I'm not sure if it was, so I don't want to say right now. That's why I'm gathering whatever facts I can, trying to figure out what happened. Neither death may be questionable." George felt regretful.

Was he spinning this too much? "Maybe it's just my lawyer's mind," he summed up, "whispering doubts where none exist."

Jerry Price pointed the two fingers that were holding the cigar at George. "Don't mess with me, George Martino. If you know something, I want to hear it right now."

George put both feet on the floor. "That's just it, Jerry. I'm not sure if I *know* anything." He placed his hands on his knees and put on his conscientious face. "What if I were to make you a deal?" The Sheriff looked skeptical as George continued, "When I know something for sure, I'll tell you."

Jerry Price crossed his forearms on the desk. "And when you do, maybe I'll tell you what I know. 'Til then, you're getting nothing from me." He leaned back and clasped his hands behind his head. "Ben won't be talking either."

13

After the Silver Foxes completed their separate inquiries, they met in Alice's apartment to bring each other up to speed. The meeting was after dinner, so she offered coffee again. Anne-Marie brought fancy little iced cakes from Bettina's Bakery.

Willard and Fred couldn't wait to tell their story this time either. So everybody sat back, drank their coffee, ate their cakes and listened. "If Brenda didn't play golf that day, where was she?" Alice asked, and George added, "Why would she lie about not just that day, but a weekly golf game?"

"Hiding something for sure," Willard said.

"Rich bi——-," Fred started to say, but Trudy stopped him in mid-speech with a look that paralyzed his lips.

"Somebody needs to follow her on what she says is her golf day," Alice said.

Anne-Marie held up a hand sparkling with diamonds. "I can do that." She smiled at George. "I feel like I haven't done a thing yet, and you've all been so productive."

Trudy and Alice glanced at each other, and each woman knew what the other was thinking. *Not Anne-Marie. She could use Brenda as a smoke screen if she needs to cover her tracks.*

Fortunately, George stepped in. "Not sure we want to risk your neck," he said to the petite Anne-Marie. "Brenda's a big gal and athletic." He grinned at the group. "I'll follow her. Use my son's old gray Honda instead of my BMW. Never been a car more inconspicuous. Might even get out my trench coat and Dad's fedora."

"Hrrrumph," Fred said, but Anne-Marie looked like she'd won Queen of the May.

"Won't that interfere with pursuing clues about Alejandro Garcia?" Alice said.

George appeared chagrined. "That went exactly nowhere. Jerry Price knew I'd been talking to one of his deputies. The Sheriff isn't going to tell me a thing until he's ready to tell it to the world. He's also forbidden his deputy to talk. Price wouldn't even say what they discovered when they checked the body shops about repairing an SUV fender."

"We could do that," Fred said, "Me and Willard."

"How you gonna get the body shop guys to talk anyway?" Charlie said. "Cops've got pull, but a couple old geezers don't."

"You leave that to us," Fred started to say, but Willard interrupted, "Charlie's got a point. Besides, we don't know that Alejandro's car was actually hit. That homeless guy saw Alejandro swerve like he was trying to avoid a collision. The guy didn't hear a crash, so there wouldn't be a mark on the dark SUV."

George nodded. "Maybe just let that one ride for a while. I'll try to find the witness and see what he can remember about what happened that night."

Alice had the impression George knew more but didn't want to say anything at this point. No matter, she'd tackle him later in case it wasn't for all ears.

"Okay, my turn," Charlie said and proceeded to relay all that happened when he waylaid Janice Cunningham at the track. By the time he'd finished every little detail, Fred was twitching with the need to speak.

"Seems like we got nothing but lying..." Fred struggled for the word, "...women."

Trudy was crocheting something large and brown as they talked. It looked like a turkey to Alice. Something for Evergreen's Thanksgiving celebration?

"I never saw Janice Cunningham visit Skilled Nursing," Trudy said. "Of course, I wasn't there all the time, and I wasn't on duty when Suzie died. But I can check the Guest Register next time I'm volunteering. All visitors have to sign in if they're coming from off-campus. Thought I'd talk with Alejandro's sister at the same time. She might know something."

Alice smiled. "Trudy, why don't you tell us what you overheard the other day?" Trudy kept it short and sweet, ending with, "Not sure there's anything to the Greg Pendergast angle, especially with Alejandro having seen a woman leaving Suzie's room. But it's worth following up, and I'll do that at church this Sunday." Alice was grateful Trudy didn't mention that she was coming too.

Charlie smiled at Trudy and said, "You're becoming our number-one spy."

Trudy kept her head down, focused on her knitting, and Alice figured he'd touched a raw nerve.

"We're all taking on spying roles, whether we like it or not," Alice said. "It's for Suzie, and we'll have to come to terms with how we feel about what we're doing once it's over. In the meantime, let's give each other all our support." She eyed Fred and Charlie, wishing they'd take more care before they said the first thing that blundered onto their tongues.

She didn't look at Anne-Marie, and she didn't mention their upcoming lunch. The widow had no idea she might be a suspect, and Alice was going to keep it that way.

Sunday rolled around, and Trudy stood in front of her bureau mirror, straightening her red felt hat with the black ribbon. Seemed like most women didn't wear hats to church anymore, and Alice probably didn't even own one. She'd show up in just her shaggy gray hair and think that was good enough. But for Trudy, hats were a sign of respect, and she couldn't imagine going to church without one.

But Alice did have a hat. There was a knock on Trudy's door, and there stood Alice in a narrow-brimmed chapeau, a pheasant feather stretching from the band back past her shoulder. Trudy wondered where it had come from. Goodwill? An old family trunk? Well, at least it was sort of a hunting hat. Very appropriate. They stepped out into the weak sunshine and headed for Trudy's bronze Taurus.

Once they arrived at the Lewiston Baptist Church, Trudy led the way inside and paused to see if Greg Pendergast was there. But he wasn't. She was feeling discouraged. All this for nothing and dragging Alice along too. Then she heard a familiar voice, and there he was, behind them.

Trudy turned, "Greg, how nice to see you. Let me introduce my friend, Alice." The two shook hands as Trudy continued. "I didn't get to thank you properly for filling in at the Information Desk."

"Not at all," he said and tried to slip by. But Trudy wasn't having any of that and walked down the aisle with him, Alice following along. Greg had no choice but to slide into a pew with Trudy beside him and Alice on the aisle.

They no sooner were seated, than the service began. There was a rousing sermon with some of Trudy's favorite hymns, but she couldn't concentrate. All she could think about was getting Greg to talk at the social after the service. Finally, the choir sang the recessional, and Trudy could take Greg by the arm. "Let me buy you a cup of coffee." They both knew the coffee would be free, as would the home-made biscuits and other goodies, but it was a common way to suggest being together. With Trudy on his arm, Greg had no choice, and off the three of them strolled to the church hall.

Trudy spotted Brenda and her husband across the room, but this was the day to focus on Greg, and she just nodded at Suzie's kin.

Alice ushered Trudy and Greg to three folding chairs in the corner, and they sat down. Trudy led the talk about inconsequential things for a while and then said, "So lovely to have a nice chat. I do miss Suzie Cunningham, don't you? She used to be full of interesting things to talk about."

Greg's eyes seemed to bug out of his head, and he literally gave a small start. Trudy smiled, "I often saw the two of you together. You must miss her as much as we do."

He stood up, spilling his napkin from his lap. "Sorry. Must get home. You know my wife isn't well." And he nearly ran out of the room.

Trudy looked at Alice. "Now isn't that interesting?" she said.

Tuesday arrived, and George could follow Brenda on her "golf day." Even though he wasn't wearing a trench coat and a fedora, he still felt like a private eye. Maybe it was the inconspicuous Honda? Anyway, he wasn't surprised when Brenda drove right by the Country Club and turned onto the back road that went to Moorestown. That road was so rarely travelled, George had to slow down and stay back so Brenda wouldn't see his ancient gray car.

He followed her up over the hill and past Junior Flint's old house, totally deserted, porch caved in, windows all broken, chimney cracked now that none of the Flint brothers were there to take care of the place. The effect was sad and lonesome, but with Junior in jail and his youngest brother in the State Mental Hospital, the two middle brothers had moved to Ohio permanently.

Too bad about Junior. For a while there, it'd seemed like he was going to straighten up. But some stranger challenged his manhood, and Junior answered the only way he knew how. The stranger grabbed a beer bottle, and Junior pulled a knife. The stranger went to the hospital, and Junior went to jail. That was the end of the Flint brothers living in their ancestral home.

Down the hollow and past where Mrs. Simmons was burned alive in her cabin. Thanks to Farnsworth's help with her will, the place belonged to Jimmy Lee Schuman. That young man had turned out to be a credit to his father after Mr. Schuman died in a mine accident. Jimmy Lee'd helped Jerry Price find out who was responsible for Mrs. Simmons' death and then turned the ruins into the Good Shepherd Kennel.

George watched Brenda zipping along in her dark-green Mercedes SUV. You'd think she'd take a less recognizable car if she wanted to slip away. Probably figured she was free and clear. Kids in school, husband at work. Back road. Who'd notice or care?

Finally Brenda got to Moorestown with George not far behind. They went straight through on Main Street. George was rubbernecking some, looking at the beautiful old brick buildings from a hundred years ago. His office used to be in that one on the corner with Euclid Avenue. A lot of those buildings were vacant now, but a few storefronts had tattoo and piercing parlors, video games or second-hand shops.

He almost missed Brenda driving onto the frontage road by the old bypass entrance. There'd been a bargain-basement gas station there for ages and what everybody around called the "No-Tell Motel." Surely she wasn't going to that sleazy place? Been sleazy since George got out of law school, probably even more now. But the Mercedes turned in, and George had to drive by, make an illegal U-turn, then hurry back to pull over and watch from across the street.

He had a clear view of Brenda steering into the parking slot farthest from the road. She got out, glanced quickly around, hurried to the last door and knocked. The door opened, and there was Lonnie Griffith, Brenda's old high school beau and captain of the football team, now a used-car dealer. Lonnie gave the parking lot the once-over, grabbed Brenda's wrist, drew her inside and shut the door.

George shook his head. So Brenda had her weekly "golf game" on the day her mother died. Of course, she'd want to hide where she really was. But was Brenda truly here with Lonnie on that day or with Suzie in Skilled Nursing?

14

WHILE GEORGE WAS BUSY INVESTIGATING Brenda and Lonnie at the No-Tell Motel, Trudy decided she couldn't wait until it was her turn to be a Volunteer. She wanted to visit the Information Desk at Skilled Nursing now and see what she could learn about visitors the day Suzie died. When she got there, a couple women she knew were on duty and chewing the fat, so it was easy for her to check the Guest Register. Janice Cunningham wasn't on it. Neither was Rodney, despite what he'd said at the funeral. But as today's Volunteers demonstrated, sometimes they got more interested in yakking to each other than in paying attention to their Information Desk duties.

Trudy waved goodbye to the women, and they barely acknowledged her departure. As soon as she had some privacy, she phoned Alice and told her what she'd discovered. "In all honesty," she said, "some of those Volunteers get so caught up in visiting together that somebody could sneak by without signing in."

"So what do we do now?" Alice asked.

"When I get a chance, I'll ask Bethanne, make it seem just chatty, see whether she knows if Janice or Rodney was there." Then Trudy went down the Skilled Nursing hall to talk with Alejandro's sister, but she wasn't there.

Alice went to bed pondering how each suspect's path seemed to just lead on and on. When were the Silver Foxes going to get closure on any of them? Math was so much more satisfying. You did the work, and you got the answer. With sleuthing, you did the work and there was just more work to be done. Kind of like housekeeping, never her number-one priority. Why couldn't people behave like numbers? It was really a pain. What had she got herself into? If it weren't that the investigation was for Suzie, she'd give up. With a long sigh, she started doing some contraction-and-release exercises in bed. Those never failed to relax her and help her get to sleep.

When Wednesday dawned, she felt reinvigorated, despite her misgivings. Outside, it was overcast and threatening rain, but inside, she felt hopeful again. She hurried to dress and get over to the Evergreen Cafe for coffee with George. But not so hurried that she didn't take some care with her appearance, choosing her brown wool skirt, matching boots and a cream-colored turtleneck with a long scarf in fall colors.

George had called to suggest a meeting right after he returned from Moorestown, and besides, she needed to know everything that had transpired with Sheriff Price. She asked herself if she should feel guilty about having side meetings with George. Did it mean she enjoyed being alone with him? Well, she had side meetings with Trudy too. Should she feel guilty about side meetings, period? *Too much introspection*, she told herself, and headed for the Cafe.

George was already there, waiting with a chocolate-dipped cruller for her. She found herself smiling at his thoughtfulness. Oh dear, what was happening to her? Best not to think about that now. Even so, she did notice how spiffy he looked in navy cords, red gingham shirt and gray V-neck sweater. Shaking her head, she focused on getting her coffee and carried it to his table.

"I didn't want to discuss what I saw in Moorestown over the phone," he said. "It's a bit intimate, and I thought we'd better get together so we didn't misunderstand each other."

For goodness sake, Alice thought, *we're grown-ups. Get on with it.* "I'm sure there's nothing you can't say to me," she said.

To her dismay, George blushed. Then he told about seeing Brenda meet Lonnie Griffith at the No-Tell Motel. "But that doesn't mean she wasn't at Evergreen with her mother on the day Suzie died," he ended and paused as if working on another angle. "I can't figure any way we could broach this topic with Lonnie. 'Awkward' doesn't begin to describe it."

"Oh dear," Alice said, "another effort without a clear conclusion."

"I know, it feels like it'll never end."

Alice felt disconcerted to think he might be having doubts like she'd had the night before, so she changed the subject. "When we all met the other evening to catch up on everyone's endeavors, it seemed like maybe you had more to say about your meeting with Jerry Price."

George blushed again, took a sip of his coffee, nearly choked and said, "I was feeling guilty about telling Jerry maybe more than I should have."

"More? What more?"

George shifted in his seat, gazed out the window at trees nearly bare of leaves, then looked at Alice. "I told him I had some reason to believe that Garcia's death might be connected to another suspicious one."

Alice couldn't believe it. "Oh, George. You didn't. You had no right."

"I was trying to get the Sheriff to open up, but I went too far." He shook his head and wrapped his arms around his torso. "I think I'm losing my courtroom skills."

Alice saw how downhearted he was and started to respond, but he continued. "Anyway, I think I fixed it. Told him it was just my lawyerly mind whispering connections where probably none existed. Made him a deal that if and when I knew something for sure, I'd tell him."

"What did he say?" Alice asked.

"What I already reported. Until I had something, I'd get nothing from him or his deputy either."

Alice put her elbows on the table and leaned her chin on her clasped hands. She sat there for a while, thinking and letting George stew. He should've known better. What was the matter with him? Did the Silver Foxes need to talk about what they could and couldn't tell others? This was pain piled on pain.

Finally she looked up and said, "Do you think Sheriff Price will try to follow up on what you told him? Will he try to find out what the other suspicious death may be?"

George's face was full of remorse. "Hope not. I left it as vague as possible. He's not going to confide in me until I confide in him." Alice started to speak, and George rushed to finish, "And I'm not going to do that until we all agree that we've got some proof, and we want him to know."

That Wednesday was full of developments, three of them revolving around lunches. Bethanne's was first. She was sitting in her car outside Lewiston High, waiting for Eden and feeling overburdened with questions about Suzie Cunningham. Trudy had asked her about

Janice Cunningham visiting the day of Suzie's death. Of course, she'd had to say she didn't know whether Rodney's wife had been there or not.

Now Eden had been pestering Greg Pendergast so much about his relationship with Suzie, he'd complained to Bethanne. This had to stop. She was going to take Eden for lunch at the Quik Treet and get her back on track.

Eden jogged down the walkway and hopped in the car. "Guess you know I only have forty-five minutes between classes, but it sure is nice to have a little time to ourselves. Seems like we're so busy, we never get to see each other like we used to."

Bethanne smiled and started the car. "I know. We used to be together almost everyday. Now we're on paths that keep us apart more than I'd like."

Eden smiled back, and they continued on to Quik Treet, catching up on each other's news.

Bethanne suggested they order take-out so they could eat in the car and save time. They got a couple burgers and fries with Cokes and sat in the parking lot just like they did in days gone by.

"You know how proud I am of you?" Bethanne asked. "You're not that fat little loser you thought you were. You've grown into a young lady with a future. Early admission to Pre-Med and in strong running for a scholarship."

Eden grinned. "You're the one who gave me the idea while we were waiting to ride the roller coaster. Remember? I said no way a girl from Happy Hours Trailer Park was gonna get a scholarship, and you said if I got good grades, I could." She patted Bethanne's arm. "Looks like maybe you were right."

"Knew you had it in you," Bethanne said. "You're smart, and you're about the most responsible person I know. Look what you've done with the EverTeens. Staff used to complain that all the girls did was hang around and flirt with the interns. Now the EverTeens do all kinds of things that let the staff focus on taking care of residents' medical needs."

It broke Bethanne's heart to see Eden grin even more, but she knew she had to get on with it. "That's why I wanted to talk with you about Greg Pendergast."

Eden scowled. "He's not what he seems to be. Something funny going on."

"You're going to ruin your good reputation around Evergreen if you keep this up," Bethanne said. "You've got to stop pestering him. Suzie Cunningham is gone, so it doesn't matter what kind of relationship they had."

"What if they were having an affair?" Eden said.

"So what if they were? That's not a reason for him to kill her." Bethanne smiled and tried to make her voice gentle. "You need a good letter of recommendation from Evergreen. I'm your friend, but I'm also the Volunteer Coordinator. I can't lie for you. And if the Director finds out what you've been doing, you could even be kicked out of EverTeens. I care about you, and I want you to be all you can be. Let this go."

Eden hung her head like she was considering what Bethanne had said. "Okay, I hear you. Let me think on this, and we'll talk again. How would that be?"

Bethanne smiled. "Just like old times."

15

MAYBE EDEN AND BETHANNE HAD to hurry through lunch at the Quik Treet, but Willard and Fred had the luxury of being retirees. After a nice midday meal at Evergreen, they took their daily naps. Then Fred drove Willard out to Great Oaks in his ancient Cadillac. They hadn't bothered to tell the Silver Foxes what they were doing. "They'd only tell us not to come out here," Fred said as he navigated the narrow county road, patched so many times the original tarmac almost disappeared. "They couldn't imagine we'd find anything, but we found the biggest clue so far, and now we're going to catch that bastard."

Willard nodded, took a swig from his Dr. Pepper, burped and wiped his mouth with the back of his hand. "You got that right. We sure had the goods on Rodney once we learned about the new highway."

Fred turned off the road and headed through tall stone pillars and down the long circular drive to the old clapboard mansion with its wrap-around porch. A seam opened in the overcast sky to let a ray of weak sunshine bounce off the multi-colored panes surrounding the windows.

"Remember those little shortbread cookies with powdered

sugar Suzie served when we played bridge out here?" Willard said. "Purely melted in your mouth."

"I remember the Tom Collins on the porch after we played," Fred said. "Sitting there, wondering how much it'd cost to screen in that damn veranda. Just about eaten alive by mosquitos." He pulled behind the house, backing and shuffling until no one could see the car unless they came within fifteen feet of it.

"You need you a new car," Willard said. "This one's like an aircraft carrier." He squirmed to pull his body upright. "Gotta expect bugs out in the country. You're getting too soft from living in air conditioning all the time."

Fred opened the car door. "Dammit, I grew up in the country. Know all about buggy evenings. Doesn't mean I have to like 'em." He zipped up his wool jacket. "Nothing wrong with this car. Keep it in tune, and it'll run forever."

Willard was still trying to heave his body out of the Caddy, but Fred was impatient. "Let's go," the dentist said. "No bugs now. We can start by the creek."

Fred took off down the gentle slope without looking back, and Willard did his best to follow, stuffing the Dr. Pepper in his jacket pocket. They walked through dry grasses and weeds to stand above the swimming hole. "Bet those Cunningham grandchildren have a ball down there when it's hot," Willard said.

Fred stooped to pick burrs out of his corduroy trousers. "Course they do. Come on, we're not going swimming this time of year." He headed upstream, away from the entrance to Great Oaks. The bank of the creek was lined with bushes and trees, most of them leafless this time of year. But there were some evergreens too, so the two men couldn't see what was ahead.

Fred was still in the lead. Suddenly, he stopped and held a hand back to keep Willard from moving forward. Voices came from the direction they were headed. The two friends began to steal as softly as they could through the brush. When the voices seemed loud enough, they stopped behind a tall pine and peeked through the branches.

Two men were hauling survey equipment through the field on the same side of the creek, away from the main road. "Mr. Rodney said one-acre lots, so that's what we're doing," said the one in the gray hunting jacket with pockets all around.

"I thought he wanted five acres for the big house," said the scrawny, younger guy in camouflage jacket and baseball cap.

The older one, who seemed to be in charge, put his hand on his hips and let out a sigh. "Like I said, we'll do that later. Let's get the smaller ones done first."

"How much you figure they're going to sell for?" said the young one.

The older man began to set up the tripod and digital station. "More'n we can afford. These here're for doctors and lawyers." He pointed to a spot on a line perpendicular to the creek. "Take the rod over there. Careful now. Don't bust the reflector."

"That Mr. Rodney, he's gonna make a heap of money," the scrawny guy said and loaded the rod on his shoulder.

"You kiddin'? He's gonna make a whole bank-full once he gets done with all that commercial development too."

Willard looked down at Fred and whispered, "See? Told you. It's always about the money."

Fred rolled his eyes. "Told you the bastard was lying."

Alice raced home from meeting with George, washed her face, put on her coat and headed for the Country Club. She didn't want to be late for her lunch with Anne-Marie. Alice already felt at a disadvantage because of the location. She didn't belong to the Club. That was never her scene, and besides, she couldn't have afforded it anyway. But it had been Anne-Marie's choice, because she was exercising in the Club gym during the morning and didn't want to travel back to town.

The retired professor drove along the winding road through the golf course, clumps of dark pines showing the only color against the gray of the bare forest limbs behind. When she got to the brownstone clubhouse, there was some brighter color from an arrangement of pumpkins and Indian corn on the stone steps leading to the entrance. But on the whole, it felt like a gray and gloomy place, matching the gray and gloomy day.

She parked and headed for the dining room, where Anne-Marie was already waiting for her. The widow seemed freshly showered, made-up and dressed. Alice wondered how she could work out all morning, get spruced up and still look like she'd only just got ready for lunch after reading a good book. Alice felt like her brown-and-cream outfit was positively dowdy beside Anne-Marie's plum-colored pantsuit with suede boots to match.

Alice let go of that notion and sat down under the hovering waiter's gaze. "Sorry to keep you waiting. Was that Tom's old SUV I saw in the parking lot? Are you driving that now?"

Anne-Marie looked disconcerted. "Gosh, no. Tom loved that car, but I hate driving anything so big. Sold it months ago." She glanced at the waiter and back at Alice. "What'll you drink? I'm having an Arnold Palmer."

Whatever that is, Alice thought and ordered, "Just water, please."

"Thanks for coming out here for lunch," Anne-Marie said. "The Club Board is meeting this afternoon. I'm Secretary, so I need to stay here all day."

"Glad to oblige," Alice said, and the two women began studying their menus. When the waiter returned, they gave their orders and chatted about Evergreen gossip. Alice didn't want to talk about where Anne-Marie was when Suzie died until it felt right.

The food arrived, and the widow picked at her Cobb salad, while Alice fell to her grilled ham steak, scalloped potatoes and succotash with gusto. She felt ravenous. Maybe it was all the emotions of her meeting with George.

They got to dessert. Anne-Marie ordered "only black coffee" and said, "Don't let me stop you. The Club has the most scrumptious lemon merengue pie ever made." Alice had never had to watch her weight and had no intention of starting now. When the pie came, it really was delicious. Anne-Marie seemed at ease, performing her favorite role as hostess, so it finally seemed the right time to talk about Suzie's death.

Alice finished her pie, took a sip of her coffee and said, "For some reason, I've been thinking lately about where I was when Suzie died." Anne-Marie appeared a little startled, and Alice rushed on. "I know it may seem morbid, but somehow it comforts me to know where I was. Like putting everything in perspective." She smiled at Anne-Marie. "Do you remember where you were? Were you here?"

Anne-Marie's eyes welled over, and she carefully wiped under them with a cambric hanky she pulled from her jacket pocket. "I'll never forget. I was putting fresh flowers on Tom's grave."

Alice felt like the world's greatest jerk for having asked, even as she was wondering how she could possibly check that alibi.

Anne-Marie's pearl-drop earrings swung back and forth as she shuddered. "Gosh, that's hard to think about. I visit his grave every week. Just need to be together for a while. I feel so alone now all the kids and grandkids are on the West Coast." Her face changed from sad to wonder. "But you know what? When I was there this week, Rodney was there too. Not at Tom's grave. At the niche where Suzie's ashes are. He was crying like a baby. Isn't that the strangest thing? I never thought he could've killed her, and that just about proves it."

16

It wasn't long before Trudy's turn at the Information Desk arrived. She was eager to try out her new plan to discover what happened on the day of Suzie's death. She'd cut the buttons off her gray Volunteer tabard and roughed up the threads so it would look like they'd torn on their own. Now she'd have an excuse to ask Bethanne for help.

She peeked through the Volunteer locker room door to make sure Bethanne was at the desk, then she rushed out, seemingly breathless and trying to button her tabard. "Oh, Bethanne, something's wrong with my tabard. I can't fasten it."

The Volunteer Coordinator smiled and told her to raise her arms. "No wonder. The buttons for both tabs are gone. The new tabards haven't come yet, but I've got some buttons we can sew on."

Trudy followed Bethanne through the locker room door to Bethanne's office in the rear, trying not to smile. There was just barely room for a desk and two visitor's chairs, but the intimacy might work to Trudy's benefit. She watched Bethanne take a tin box out of her desk drawer and open it to show extra buttons, as well as needles and thread. Trudy realized her plan had a weakness. What if Bethanne handed her the sewing materials and left her to fix her tabard? She smiled. "Can you spare a few minutes to help me? If we sew buttons together, it'll take half the time." To Trudy's relief, Bethanne agreed, and they sat down on opposite sides of the desk, each working on a button.

Trudy decided to raise the topic of what happened in the hallway first. "I miss seeing Alejandro's smiling face. The residents do too. He just pepped everybody up with his kindness and caring."

Bethanne licked her thread and fit it through the eye of the needle. Her face looked sad. "Me too. He was very special."

"What's happened to his sister? I haven't seen her for a while."

Bethanne looked up as if puzzling over why Trudy would ask. "Yes, we're missing her too. They were both so positive. She's been given compassionate leave, and she took Alejandro's ashes to Guatemala. She should be back after Christmas. Why? Do you need to see her?"

Trudy tried not to show her disappointment. "No, just wondering. She was always so dedicated." She paused and concentrated on her button for a couple seconds. "I'm glad we get to have this time together. I'm a little troubled by something I saw the other day and didn't know whether to talk to you or not. Maybe losing these buttons is a signal I should."

Bethanne nodded her encouragement, and Trudy said, "I had occasion to come by the Information Desk the other day, and the two Volunteers acted like I wasn't even there. Don't want to name names, but they were more interested in talking to each other than making sure every visitor signed in."

Bethanne glanced up from her sewing. "I haven't seen that, but of course, the Volunteers would do the right thing when I show up."

"That got me to thinking," Trudy said. "Did no one visit Suzie

Cunningham the afternoon she died? Was she all alone? So I checked the guest register, and no one was signed in for her. Not even her husband, but he said at the funeral that he was with her."

Bethanne wound thread around the base of her sewing to strengthen the button's connection and prepared to knot the thread and cut it. "I wouldn't be surprised if the Volunteers just let Rodney pass if he came often and they knew who he was. They're not supposed to do that, but I can see it happening."

"Then anybody could have been in Suzie's room," Trudy said. "Friends, family, anybody." She finished her button and started putting the tabard on.

Bethanne rose, put the needles and thread back in the box, then slipped it into the drawer. "Now you've got me concerned. I'll ask the staff."

The two women exited the locker room, and Bethanne escorted Trudy to the Information Desk. "Sorry we're a little late," Bethanne said to the Volunteers waiting there. "We had to fix Trudy's tabard, but she's here now, and you can take off. Thanks for your patience."

Trudy tried not to let her disappointment show as she took her place at the desk. If Bethanne learned anything from the staff, how could she find out what it was?

While Trudy was walking home after her worrisome talk with Bethanne, Eden was climbing into Jimmy Lee's SUV. She reached back to scratch Flossie's bum. The dog was lying quietly, but the attention brought her tail to thumping the floor. "Thanks for picking me up after school," Eden said. "I wanted to ask your advice while we drive to Evergreen."

It felt good to hear him say, "Sure thing. Ain't that always been part of who we are?"

She smiled. "Yep, and now I need your help. Bethanne's after me to leave this Greg Pendergast thing alone. She's afraid the Director will find out what I've been doing, and I'd end up in trouble. Maybe even lose my recommendation from Evergreen for a University scholarship."

Jimmy Lee steered the car through day's end traffic, while Eden inspected a sky ready to rain. When he got to a red light, he turned to her. "Did anything come of your suspicions?" He shook his head. "Nope. Not one thing."

"What if they *were* having an affair?" Eden said. "She really perked up when he was near, and he made a special effort to spend time with her."

The light changed to green, and Jimmy Lee started off again. "So what? I perk up when we're together, and we're not having an affair. Just means we enjoy each other's company. Probably the same with Miz Cunningham and Mr. Pendergast."

Eden was silent, her thoughts racing back and forth between different interpretations of what they'd seen. They were nearing the Evergreen campus when she spoke up again. "Bethanne says I could be kicked out of EverTeens if I get caught. But that's not a good enough reason if there really was something funny going on."

Jimmy Lee pulled into a parking slot and shifted in his seat to face her. "Eden, all you got is that wonderful imagination. Sometimes it helped you a lot, but it got you in trouble too." Flossie stood up, ready to get out and get going. He reached back to lay a gentling hand on her shoulders. "You ain't got proof of nothing," he said. "Bethanne's right. Leave go."

Eden started to speak, but he raised a forefinger to her lips and said, "It's the right thing to do all round." Then it seemed like a door opened in his mind. "Is it something else? Something you ain't talked about?"

Eden fidgeted against the seat and looked out the window at raindrops starting to fall. He reached over, put a hand to her chin and turned her face to look at his. "What is it?" he said. "Nothing you can't tell me."

She was surprised to find tears begin running down her cheeks. It felt like a door opened in her own mind, thoughts racing back to the time Jeffries and Marlene tried to trick her into making child porn. She'd told Bethanne and the cops what happened, but she'd never told anyone how that made her feel, cheap and totally unable to trust older men. But now she wanted to tell Jimmy Lee.

She leaned against the far window, not wanting the comfort of his arms, needing distance but also needing to tell the one person she knew wouldn't judge and would try to understand.

When she finished, he reached out a hand to take hers. "Do you think that's why you're suspicious of Pendergast? 'Cause of what happened years ago?"

She felt salt drying on her cheeks. "Dunno. Maybe." She tried to smile but knew it was pretty weak. "Maybe I can't see anything but men taking advantage of women."

Jimmy Lee smiled. "Did I ever take advantage of you?"

"No, but we were young. You weren't a man."

He smiled again. "Well, I am now. And here's what I think. Let's just leave this alone unless we learn otherwise. Time enough to act then. Can you do that?"

Eden tried to smile back, but she still couldn't make it happen. She felt relieved to have told him and to know he understood. But she still couldn't let go of her distrust of Pendergast. Not yet, anyway. "Okay," she said.

Bethanne hurried away from the Information Desk, berating herself for not following through with the nursing staff before. True, she'd tried to talk with Alejandro's sister about what he saw in the hallway, but she'd been too late. Elena Garcia had left for Guatemala almost immediately after the funeral. Bethanne felt like she'd also dropped the ball about what had happened inside Miz Cunningham's room.

Now Trudy was asking if anyone visited Miz Cunningham despite there being no one registered for that day. She'd also asked about Alejandro's sister. The Volunteer Coordinator stopped in her tracks. Why was Trudy asking all these questions? She was probably the most diligent Volunteer, but she was also snoopy. Was Trudy just being her usual snoopy self, or was there something more to it? Well, one thing at a time.

Bethanne went down the Skilled Nursing hallway to the nursing desk. Fortunately, Sally Fragale was on duty. Not only was Sally about the most conscientious of all the nursing staff, she was also more than an acquaintance, if less than a friend. Bethanne felt comfortable asking her some questions.

"Got a few moments?" Bethanne said. "I need your input."

Sally called one of her assistants over to sit at her place and led Bethanne to the nurse's lounge behind the desk. They stood facing each other just inside the door. "What is it?" Sally asked. "How can I help?"

Bethanne smiled. "It's come to my attention that some of the Volunteers don't sign in all the visitors for our residents. I was wondering if you'd noticed anything like that."

Sally shook her head. "Not really. Visitors come and go, but we don't know if they're registered or not."

"Not your responsibility. I'm just trying to find out if I have a problem with guest registration." Bethanne crossed her arms. "I know this is weird, but I've been asked about visitors to Suzie Cunningham on the day she died. Were you on duty that day?"

"Gosh, that's been a while. And we were so busy trying to save her life."

Bethanne tried to keep her voice from sounding like an inquisition. "What about her husband? Was he there?"

"Oh yes, we had to ask him to leave so we could do our best for Miz Cunningham."

"Anybody else? A woman maybe?"

Sally's face showed regret. "Maybe. I honestly don't know. All my attention was on Miz Cunningham."

Another thought came to Bethanne. "When you got there, was there anything unusual? What was Mr. Cunningham doing?"

"Now that you mention it, he was bending over to pick up a pillow off the floor. I asked him to leave so we could do our job, and he dropped it on the chair. Then he waited out in the hall until the doctor pronounced Miz Cunningham deceased."

Bethanne was almost holding her breath. "And when he came back?"

"He was sobbing like his heart would break."

17

CHARLIE WAS STANDING ON A LADDER, helping Trudy attach Thanksgiving decorations to the central chandelier in the Independent Living dining room. Trudy had devised a festoon of pilgrim hats and pumpkins made of crepe paper and colored cardboard. It really was pretty, he thought, but it sure was the blazes to put it up where she wanted, the chandelier as the center of radiating lines out to the room's pillars and corners. And she didn't want the tape or wires to show, so that was even more of a challenge. Still, he liked lending Trudy a hand. She was so creative and always helpful to others. Time she got a little help of her own.

He peeked down at the other women on the decorating committee, spread around the room putting tiny crocheted turkeys and mini-pumpkins on every table. Trudy's big crocheted turkey was already on the dessert buffet, surrounded by artificial fall leaves in all the colors of autumn. Trudy handed him the last festoon for the chandelier, and he reached up to attach it to the base with frosted tape, so it wouldn't show.

Something happened, and Charlie felt himself tumbling through the air. Him, an athlete all his life, but somehow his foot slipped, or he lost his balance. That was his last thought until he woke up in the hospital.

"Damn fool," Fred said. "What was a man your age doing up on a ladder? What do you think we have maintenance men for?"

Charlie tried to respond, but his head hurt too much. It seemed to be restrained in a frame. And there was some kind of cast on his left leg. He was flat on his back. Fortunately, Fred was standing by the bed, so Charlie could look up at him. But when Wilbur spoke, Charlie couldn't see him at all. He must be somewhere else in the room.

"Shut up," the big man said to Fred. "You never know when to stop running your mouth."

Fred moved from the bedside toward where Willard's voice came from. "Don't tell me to shut up, you tub of ...."

"That's enough," came a voice from what seemed to be the door to the hall. "Time for you boys to leave. Mr. Coleman has another visitor." The voice came into view and revealed itself to be coming from a nurse dressed in blue pajamas with apples printed all over. At least they looked like pajamas. Whatever happened to nurses in starched white dresses and caps? That uniform implied authority. But this gal had authority too, even in her apple pajamas, and she shooed Fred and Willard out the door.

The nurse checked the frame around his head. "Let's keep our neck still for a few more days, hmmmm?" Why did nurses always say "we"? She wasn't in that contraption, he was.

Then the nurse was gone, and soft footsteps approached the bed. A vase of flowers appeared with two hands he knew. A face peeked around, spectacles slightly askew with crinkly eyes ashine. Trudy. Dear Trudy had come. His heart smiled and then fell. He felt so ashamed.

She put the vase on the bedside table. "Oh Charlie, you missed the most wonderful Thanksgiving dinner. I came with you in the ambulance, but they wouldn't let me stay once you went off for a CT scan. The Evergreen Director told me to go back home, but it wasn't the same without you next day at our Thanksgiving table. We had turkey with all the trimmings, and your decorations looked just grand..."

"Not my decorations," he interrupted. "You made them. I just helped hang them up."

Trudy was standing with her hands on the raised bed rails. "All my fault you fell. I distracted you just as you were reaching for the chandelier base, and you lost your balance." She put a fingertip to the corner of her eye, and it came away damp. "I'll never forgive myself."

Charlie reached up to put his hand on top of hers. "But I forgive you. And that's what counts."

Alice again assembled the Silver Foxes in the Game Room. Ever since that day with Brenda filling in for her mother, they'd been playing bridge with a dummy. Now Charlie was in the hospital, so there'd be no bridge for a while. Besides, it was clear their hearts weren't really in it anyway. Maybe they never would be.

Everybody had been to visit Charlie, some of them more than once. He was coming back to Evergreen soon, to the Skilled Nursing facility until he was well enough to move to Assisted Living or even directly back to his apartment. That was a decision which would have to wait until the staff saw how well the stable fracture in his shin bone healed and responded to rehab. Old bones didn't heal as quickly or as well as young bones.

Alice watched the Foxes as they picked up hot drinks from the buffet and came to sit around the coffee table. She'd brought assorted sweets from Bettina's Bakery. That definitely went over better than store-bought cookies. Now they gazed at her expectantly, like she was the leader, even if they did most of the legwork.

"Let me start off by suggesting we meet here every week during our normal bridge time," Alice said. "So much is happening, we need to report regularly and plan next steps." She smiled to soften her next remark. "And we probably need to set up some guidelines for what we should and shouldn't do."

Fred's dander was obviously up. "You coming down on me and Willard?"

"Well, we need it," Willard said. "We been holding back, and that's no good."

"Holding back?" George said. "Something besides what you learned from your accountant buddy?"

Willard slurped his coffee and reached for a chocolate eclair. "Yep." He looked ashamed, and Alice wondered if the eclair was solace.

"Willaaaard," Fred strung out his name in admonition.

"If we're going to figure out what's going on, we can't have secrets," Alice said. "Either we're a team, or we're not. Nothing half-way."

Trudy nodded. "We have to be a team. That was Charlie's idea, and it's a good one." She glanced at Willard and Fred. "I haven't told everything I know either, so if you want, I'll start."

Fred lurched forward in his chair. "No, dammit, I'll start. Me and Willard went out to Great Oaks and saw a survey team measuring out one-acre plots. Rodney's already on the move."

"When was this?" George asked.

"A while back. We didn't say anything because so much has been happening that we didn't all get together." George looked skeptical, and Fred rushed on, "No lie, that's it."

Alice turned to George. "Is that legal? Surveying Suzie's property now? Surely the will hasn't been probated."

George's shoulders rose and fell in a brief shrug. "Seems to me it all depends. Brenda can make plans for the house all she wants to, as long as she doesn't put those plans into action before probate. Rodney can give his daughters an advance payment for the land, and Brenda can use that to buy Penelope out. Rodney can survey that land as long as he doesn't start to sell lots. I suppose somebody could challenge him on this, but the girls are the ones with vested interests. Maybe all three have worked this out to their mutual satisfaction. Of course, if it were to turn out that there are other parties who can contest the will, then all bets are off until those disputes are resolved in probate."

"Damn," Fred said. "Trust the lawyers to make it complicated."

"Knock it off," Willard said. "That was a good question and a useful answer. Who else might have a vested interest? Any siblings or cousins around?"

Trudy looked up from her knitting. "Not that Suzie mentioned. She always said she inherited the land free and clear." The grandmother surveyed the group with raised eyebrows. "My turn now?" Heads nodded, and she relayed what she'd learned about Greg Pendergast's strange relationship with Suzie.

"Is that all?" Anne-Marie said, "Why didn't you mention this before? I knew all about it. They were good friends, went to the same church. Maybe they were a little sweet on each other, but goodness sake, she was divorced, and his wife just isn't with it anymore. She's going to be admitted to Memory Care any day now. So what if Suzie and Greg were a comfort to each other?"

Fred mimicked Anne-Marie. "Is that all? How do you know there wasn't more to it? You already said Suzie was hurting for money. What if she was giving Greg cash to help out with his wife's care?" He leered. "Besides, he's younger than Suzie. Probably one of those damn predators that go after older women."

Anne-Marie opened her mouth to respond, but Willard butted in. "I haven't wanted to relay this, but if we're talking about a predator going after Suzie and maybe killing her..." He paused like he was thinking about whether to mention something or not. Willard took in a big breath and blew it out before continuing. "Okay. I happen to know Greg's insurance business is about to go bust. I still do his taxes, and the man's in deep trouble."

"See?" Fred said to Anne-Marie. "You always want to believe the best of your friends. You need to wise up, sister."

"That's enough, Fred," George said. "If we're a team, we don't talk to each other like that."

Anne-Marie favored George with her most gracious smile of thanks.

Fred fiddled with his hearing aid and muttered, "Sorry."

This seems as good a time as any, Alice thought. "Speaking of talking to each other," she said, "we need to discuss what we say to people outside the Silver Foxes." She purposely didn't look at George. "One of us shared information in order to get information, and it didn't work. Now we have to worry about what this outside person will do with what he learned."

Fred looked ready to burst with the need to know who did it, and Alice tried to head him off. "Let's not focus on who, let's focus on what."

George raised a hand. "I'll fess up. It was me. I told Sheriff Price about the possible link between Suzie's and Alejandro's deaths."

"God dammit," Fred said. "Who died and put you in charge?"

Trudy's frown made Fred's head hang. "That's not helping," she said. "What's done is done. The question is what do we do now?"

"I think I headed Price off," George said. "Told him it was just my lawyerly imagination running wild. If we do find a connection, we best tell him though."

"In the meantime," Alice said, "nobody talks to anybody outside the Silver Foxes unless we all agree it makes sense." She looked around the group, and every head was nodding, even Fred's.

"So what about loose ends?" Trudy prodded. "I've got a couple. I thought it might be a good idea to talk with Alejandro's sister..."

Her face took on a momentary scowl when Fred butted in, "Yeah, good idea. We should've followed up on this before. Just like we should've followed up on repairs to an SUV. Do an end-run around the Sheriff. What do you say? Me and Willard can check out every body shop in the county."

"Probably too late to find out anything now," George said. "But what the heck, give it a try." Everyone agreed, and he turned to Trudy. "So what did you find out from the sister?"

"Nothing. She got compassionate leave and left right after the funeral to take Alejandro's ashes back to Guatamala."

Fred groaned. "See? We're letting stuff slip through the cracks."

Trudy continued as if he'd never put in his two cents' worth. "I also checked the Guest Register, and Janice isn't on it for the day Suzie died. Doesn't mean she wasn't there though. I've seen Volunteers so busy talking to each other that they didn't sign visitors in." She paused to make sure everyone was listening. "But Rodney was there that day even though he didn't register. I asked Bethanne, and she confirmed it with the nursing staff."

Anne-Marie sat forward. "I know all the Cunninghams. None of them would kill Suzie. Rodney was weeping at her cemetery niche just the other day. I loved Suzie as much as any of you, but I just can't see Janice killing her. Nothing to gain. She had Rodney and everything she wanted in life."

"Bullshit," Fred said. "Rodney was still in love with Suzie. Him crying beside the urn of her ashes just proves it. Maybe Janice had to get her rival out of the way."

Alice ignored his outburst. "Okay, let's assume for a moment that it wasn't Janice. If she's not the woman Alejandro saw, who was it?"

"Brenda?" George said. "After Fred and Willard found out she wasn't at the Club on her golf day, I followed her to that old motel outside Moorestown," He seemed embarrassed. "She meets Lonnie Griffith on Tuesdays."

Anne-Marie gasped. "You don't mean it! Lonnie?" She shrugged. "Well, okay. They were sweethearts in high school." She looked around at Suzie's friends. "But kill her own mother? Not very likely. I'll take Brenda to lunch and make sure she was with Lonnie." Her face turned smug. "None of the Cunninghams did it. Just wait, I'll prove it."

"Hold on," Willard said. "What about Penelope?"

Fred's disdain was palpable "I seriously doubt she's got the guts."

Anne-Marie gave them both a look that would freeze a boiling egg. "Okay, I'll prove that too. None of the Cunninghams did it."

A lot of stress and strife, Alice thought, but at least everyone was passionately involved now.

Another idea came to her, this one about Anne-Marie's relationship with the Cunninghams. They came from the same background, and they were clearly friends. Anne-Marie might bend over backwards to prove any of them innocent or even, God forbid, tell them what the Silver Foxes were finding out. On the other hand, who else had a "in" with the Cunninghams, so they'd feel comfortable opening up?

Alice looked at Anne-Marie through slitted eyes, just like she'd looked at Rodney during his funeral oration. How much could she trust her?

18

THE NEXT DAY, GEORGE DROVE OUT to the scene where Alejandro's car had hurtled over the embankment. He knew it was a long shot, finding the homeless man still camped above, but George needed to know that for sure. He got out of his BMW and hiked up the hill to where the camp had been.

He'd worn his old saddle shoes just in case it was muddy, but he was lucky. It'd been fairly dry the last few days, and his favorite footwear was spared. He felt guilty about being so concerned with his appearance, but that had been part of his stock-in-trade as a trial lawyer, and he was too old to change now.

As expected, he found the campsite long abandoned, ashes from the man's fire scattered and only faint marks left on the tree bark where his tarp had been tied. Time to move on to the next step in his investigation.

Back to Lewiston to check with the Salvation Army, churches and other institutions that tried to help the increasing number of folks out of work and out of a home. He trekked from one to the other without success until he ended up at the Catholic Church. Every evening, they set up cots in their gymnasium so homeless men could sleep and get a good breakfast. Then the men had to vacate the premises before seven-thirty, because the school kids needed the place for gym class.

George parked his car in St. Mary's lot and got out with a sigh. He was raised Catholic, but he hadn't been to mass in years. Quit going to confession even before that. He'd been hoping he'd find out something at one of the other homeless institutions and avoid coming back to his old church. But now he had to suck it up and do the right thing.

He walked through familiar halls to the gym, where he found a nun tidying up after the kids. He didn't have a hat on, but he felt like he needed to take one off, so ingrained were the habits of long ago. "Excuse me, Sister, I'm trying to locate a homeless man, and I was hoping you could help."

She turned, a middle-aged woman dressed in a simple black suit with a white blouse and a large cross around her neck. What a change from the long black habits, wimples and rosaries cascading from roped waists when he went to St. Mary's. "Yes?" she said. "I have a few moments before the women's auxiliary comes to lend a hand. What do you want to know?"

He was glad he'd put on a tie with his zip-up jacket. "I'm sorry to bother you, but I'm trying to find the man who witnessed the accident where Alejandro Garcia was killed. The man was camping out in the woods and saw Alejandro's car go over the embankment. Has that man ever been here?"

Her face turned sad, and she leaned on her push-broom. "Oh, Alejandro. Such a sweet man. He and his sister were parishioners here. She's out of the country now, but when I saw her at the funeral, she was only half herself without him."

The nun looked like she was going to say more about the victim and his sister, but George needed her to focus while they still had time before her helpers arrived. "What about the witness to the accident?" he said. "The homeless man, did he ever come to your shelter?"

The nun smiled and shook her head as if with memories. "You mean Philip Elliott. Hard to believe he used to be an altar boy at St. Mary's, he fell down so far. Took to drink, lost his job, wife divorced him and kept the kids. Goes to AA but keeps falling off the wagon. Never gets through all Twelve Steps."

George was dumbfounded. "How do you know Philip Elliott is the man I mean?"

Her smile was even broader. "He used to come here and talk about the accident. Said he saw the whole thing, tried to help, but it was too late."

"You sound like he doesn't come anymore."

"No. Afraid he's one of the lost ones. Left town a while ago. Said he was going to go get some Florida sunshine. Hitched a ride with a man he knew who was driving down there."

George tried not to let his disappointment show. "Did Elliott say anything else about the accident?" He kept the question open-ended just like his lawyerly training told him, trying not to lead her answer.

The door to the gym opened, and the nun turned. A group of women entered, carrying folding cots, pillows and blankets. "Sister?" George prompted.

She turned back. "Philip did say he didn't like to tell the Sheriff, because he wasn't a hundred percent sure. But he was pretty sure it was a woman who drove Alejandro off the road."

About the same time that George set out looking for the witness to Alejandro's crash, Anne-Marie phoned Brenda Cunningham. She chatted for a while and then said, "Have the architect and interior designer come through with plans for Great Oaks? I'd love to see what you're going to do with that beautiful place."

"You bet." Brenda's voice positively glowed. "And I have great news. Dad's paying us for almost all the land, so I'll easily have enough money to buy out Penelope. Lots of weeping and wailing, you can imagine. But in the end, she decided she needs money more than she needs a B&B. So we're spared that embarrassment, thank God. No strangers sleeping in Momma's bed."

That was all Anne-Marie needed. She invited Brenda to lunch at the Country Club in a couple days' time and asked Suzie's daughter to bring the plans, so she could hear all about them. Anne-Marie could hardly wait until the day of her triumph, when she proved once and for all that no Cunningham was involved in Suzie's death. When that day came, she put on one of her most stylish outfits and drove out to the Club.

They both had Cobb salads and no dessert. By the time Brenda spread the plans out on the table, the dining room was mostly empty, and they could talk freely. As Anne-Marie expected, the plans were exquisite. Brenda had wonderful taste and money to match, so Great Oaks would be taken back to its glory days but with contemporary touches.

When Anne-Marie had finished her genuine if extravagant praise, she suggested they take a second cup of coffee in the lounge, knowing it would be empty that time of day. The younger woman was seemingly so enthralled with being the center of attention that the always-busy Brenda forgot any other obligations she might have had and practically skipped to the lounge.

Once they were settled on a couch with their coffees and the door shut, Anne-Marie was ready with her strategy. "I just love what you're going to do with that house. It'll be a showplace for sure. You can put it on the Garden Club list for their annual Open House Tour. I wouldn't be surprised if you don't get written up in magazines and asked to come on local television."

The much larger Brenda simpered at the petite Anne-Marie. "Do you really think so? I'd love to be on the Tour. I'm always on the organizing committee, but our house hasn't been up to that standard."

"Well, it will now, sweetie." Anne-Marie sipped her coffee. "Probably a good thing you're moving to the country anyway."

Brenda frowned. "Sorry, I don't understand."

Anne-Marie shifted in her seat, so she could face Brenda. "The privacy will do you good."

Brenda's frown deepened. "Whatever do you mean?"

"Please don't get upset. A little bird told me they saw your Mercedes at that old motel outside Morristown." Brenda turned red and started to reply, but Anne-Marie kept going, her voice hushed with sincerity. "I'm on your side in this. Let me help. Honey, you've got to be more discrete. When you move to the country, it's the ideal excuse to get some kind of nondescript, rural car that won't be so obvious. And you can come and go without so many people taking notice."

Brenda's mouth opened and closed. Her eyes blinked like the shutters on a ship's signal lamp sending a desperate message for help. Then to Anne-Marie's surprise, Brenda slumped and broke down, sobbing so loud the older woman was afraid someone would hear and come see what was the matter. Anne-Marie took a packet of Kleenex from her purse — no need to risk one of her cambric hankies — passing tissues one by one until Brenda calmed down.

"Oh sweetie," Anne-Marie said, "I never meant to upset you like this. I just wanted to give you a warning and some advice about how to go on. I'd never have brought this up if I'd known how much it would hurt you."

Brenda wiped the last of the smeared mascara from her cheeks and hiccuped a couple times. "It's not about somebody seeing my car at that motel. You're right, we need to be more careful, and we can do that." She started to cry again, and Anne-Marie placed a hand on her arm in an effort to soothe her.

"It's bigger than that," Brenda said. "That's where I was when Momma died. They tried to call me on my cellphone, but I'd turned it off." She pivoted toward Anne-Marie. "Sure, Momma had heart palpitations, but nobody thought she was going to die, not even the doctor. She was supposed to come home the very next day."

Anne-Marie patted her arm, trying to give comfort. "I know, honey, I know. We none of us expected it."

Brenda's eyes begged understanding. "I just needed some comfort from Lonnie. Get away for a while and..." She shrugged and looked embarrassed. "Well, you know. But I failed Momma, and it's tearing me up."

19

WHILE GEORGE AND ANNE-MARIE were investigating leads, Trudy was knitting beside Charlie's bed. The frame around his head had been removed, but he'd have a big collar supporting his neck for a while. The good news was he'd be returning to Evergreen tomorrow. It'd be so much easier visiting him in Skilled Nursing. Charlie let out a fluffling snore, and she smiled to hear a sound she'd missed ever since Edward died.

Her attention switched to Greg Pendergast. Despite what Anne-Marie had said at the meeting, Trudy felt this was a mystery still to be resolved. She'd seen there was something between Greg and Suzie at church. She'd tried more than once to get him to talk about it, but he kept brushing her off. What about Fred's idea? Was Suzie giving Greg money? Was Greg a predator? How could she find out? Sam Farnsworth was the lawyer for the estate. He'd have access to her bank accounts. But she hardly knew Farnsworth. Besides, there was no reason on God's green earth that he'd share such information with her. Or with George, either, for that matter. That sort of thing was definitely confidential.

She had another thought. Anne-Marie had said Greg's wife was going to be admitted to Evergreen's Memory Care. And soon.

Was Suzie's money paying for that? Trudy wondered how far gone Mrs. Pendergast was. Did she wander in and out of lucidity? If Trudy visited her now and then, would she respond to questions? And if she did, could Trudy believe what she said?

Trudy wasn't the only one thinking about Greg Pendergast. Despite what she'd told Bethanne and Jimmy Lee, Eden couldn't let go of her nagging suspicions about his furtive visits to Miz Suzie's bedside. She thought back to the times her friend Ray-Jean broke into other people's houses and how she herself had got into the Gravesley's house when Ray-Jean died so mysteriously. What if she broke into Pendergast's house when she knew he'd be volunteering at Evergreen?

The idea gave her goosebumps. If she got caught, she could kiss the chance of a University scholarship goodbye for sure. All she'd worked for, wasted. Letting down Bethanne, who'd believed in her when everybody else thought she was nothing but trailer trash. And failing Jimmy Lee, a guy so religious he'd wanted to be a preacher until he discovered he didn't really have the Call. He probably couldn't even conceive of what she was contemplating. No, there had to be some other way, but what?

Willard and Fred had finished a round of golf when they saw Anne-Marie and Brenda embracing in the parking lot. Brenda looked like she'd been put through the wringer, and Anne-Marie gave the impression she'd succeeded beyond her wildest dreams.

Fred pointed at Anne-Marie as she got in her car and drove off. "Probably can't wait to tell us how she's proved once and for all that none of the Cunninghams did it."

"You believe that?" Willard asked and chugged down most of his Dr. Pepper.

"Don't believe a word that comes out of her mouth, or Brenda's either. Just 'cause somebody says something doesn't mean it's true."

"Rodney's already dividing up house plots. Commercial plots next, I bet." Willard grinned and started to sing, "Money, money, money..."

"Shut up about the money. We need proof. We drove all over the damn county. Talked to every body shop. No record of Rodney getting his SUV fixed." Fred squinted. "Bet he paid 'em off to keep mum."

Willard huffed, "Like I said before, the two cars probably didn't hit. The SUV came over the line. Alejandro swerved and lost control."

"Or we went around the body shops too late to get any information."

"Maybe it wasn't Rodney. Could've been somebody else did it. "

"Bullshit," Fred said. "Rodney's guilty, and he's been lying ever since the funeral. Question is, what do we do about it? How do we find out what really happened?"

Willard took the last swig of his Dr. Pepper. "Okay," he groaned. "We need us a spy."

The first chance she got after talking with the nurse about who visited Suzie Cunningham, Bethanne checked the log of Volunteers for who was working the day she died. She phoned the two women and asked them to come early for a short meeting before they came on duty next time.

Her little cubbyhole at the back of the Volunteer locker room was just right for what she had in mind. When the day came, she rearranged the two metal folding chairs in front of her desk so they'd all be sitting close together. Bethanne wanted them to feel just a little uncomfortable. They were in their thirties, and she needed them aware of the gap with her in age and status. When the knock on her door came, she called out "Come in" but didn't rise.

Janie Myers and Sherry Brown came in looking a little apprehensive, and that suited Bethanne just fine. She motioned to th · ǝ chairs and said, "Have a seat." The lack of her usual warmth with Volunteers seemed to put them even more off-balance. She let the silence drag out some before speaking.

"It pains me to bring this up, but I've learned that one or more visitors came to Suzie Cunningham's room without registering the day she died. The day you two were working." The two women gaped at each other, wide-eyed. Then they looked at Bethanne and swallowed. Bethanne went on before they could say anything. "That blunder could get us all in trouble if anyone wanted to look into Miz Cunningham's passing. Or the death of any other resident for that matter."

Sherry appeared downcast. "I'm so sorry, Miz Swanson."

"It won't happen again," Janie added.

Bethanne gave them a tepid smile. "I'm counting on that, and to make sure, I'm going to assign you to different time slots so your friendship doesn't interfere with your duties." They gave every appearance of being abashed, and she continued, "Nothing wrong with friendship, but I need you to focus on what you're here for, okay?"

Janie nodded, and Sherry said, "Yes, ma'am."

Now Bethanne smiled. "You're both good Volunteers, and I know I can depend on you." She paused. "I need you to think back to that day. Who came to visit Miz Cunningham?"

Sherry crossed her legs and frowned. "Gosh, it's hard to remember that far back."

Janie looked like she was searching every inch of her memory. "The daughter, I think. She walked by us."

Sherry's voice sounded guilty. "I guess we got so used to family coming that we just let them pass without registering. Dumb, huh?"

Bethanne nodded. "Which daughter? Brenda?"

"Is that the older one?" Janie asked, and Bethanne nodded again. "No," Janie said, "Not her, the younger one."

"Penelope?" Bethanne prodded.

"Yes, that's the one."

Bethanne smiled again, wanting them to feel rewarded. "The nursing staff said Mr. Cunningham was there too."

Janie smiled back. "That's right. He arrived after his daughter got there. Maybe twenty, thirty minutes later."

Bethanne nodded. "He was still in the room when the medical staff ran in to try to save his wife. But Penelope wasn't there. Where'd she go? Did you see her leave?"

Sherry and Janie looked at each other with open mouths.

"I don't know where she went," Janie said.

"Didn't see her leave," Sherry said. "Must've gone out another door."

Jimmy Lee passed Bethanne's meeting with Janie and Sherry on his way with Flossie for their visits in Skilled Nursing. A couple residents had signed up to say they didn't want a dog to come by, but the rest welcomed Flossie like she was their own. The German Shepherd naturally loved people, and she'd learned to be gentle in demonstrating that feeling.

Like he did at every room, Jimmy Lee knocked on Mr. Windom's door and said, "Flossie's here." Mr. Windom's voice was full of pleasure. "Come on in." They walked over to the bed, and Flossie put her head up by Mr. Windom's hand. He rubbed between her ears, telling her how beautiful she was and smiling all the while.

Greg Pendergast drew his cart up to the door and saw Flossie was there. "I'll come back when you don't have company," he said. Mr. Windom thanked him for his consideration and kept on caressing Flossie as if that touch was just as good as medicine.

Jimmy Lee asked Mr. Windom how he was doing. Flossie's master knew to be careful not to go too far in his inquiries, because not all residents in this wing would get better. Happily, Mr. Windom said he'd be going home soon. After they'd visited for a while, Jimmy Lee went on to the next room and then the next, each one a variation on the time he'd spent with Mr. Windom.

As he and Flossie headed back to his SUV in the Evergreen parking lot, Jimmy Lee was thinking about Romans 12:13, "Share with the Lord's people who are in need." That was the verse which had appeared when he let his Bible fall open one day, seeking guidance about what to do next. He'd completed all his goals at the property Miz Simmons had left him, but he couldn't shake the feeling that there was more he was supposed to do. He began to meditate on that verse, and it came to him that he should train gentle Flossie to be a therapy dog. It'd taken a long time, but it was surely what God had in mind for them both.

Jimmy Lee pulled out a jug of water and a bowl from the back of the SUV and gave Flossie a drink and a biscuit before loading her inside. Then he got in the driver's seat and headed out of the parking lot. The early December sun was starting to set, even though it was just after 4:30. Not really dark yet, but threatening rain. Jimmy Lee could see someone standing at the bus stop down the street. When he got closer, he realized it was Greg Pendergast, so he pulled over. "Mr. Pendergast, can I give you a lift somewhere?"

"I don't like to impose, but it sure would help. I left my car at Mike's garage, and I need to get there before five."

Jimmy Lee was wondering why Pendergast didn't call a taxi, but his momma had taught her children not to be nosy. "Hop in," he said and moved a couple dog-breeder magazines from the passenger seat into the slot of his door.

Flossie came forward, and Pendergast reached back to pet her. "That sure is some dog you got. Hardly a resident who doesn't feel better once she's come by."

Jimmy Lee smiled and turned the corner. "I think she gets as much out of it as the residents. Flossie is a bundle of love and needs to share it."

"Suzie Cunningham definitely felt that," Pendergast said and then crushed his lips together like he was holding some emotion back.

"No question Flossie misses *her*," Jimmy Lee said. "That woman was a dog's best friend. Animals can sense what kind of person someone is. One in a million, Miz Cunningham. I still remember her in my prayers."

"Don't think she knew how purely kind she was," Pendergast responded. "Always helping others, never thinking of herself. A true Christian lady."

Jimmy Lee stopped for a red light and turned to look at Pendergast. "You say that like you've had some experience of it." He felt appalled at himself. Whatever had compelled him to say such a personal thing? He was ready to apologize when the light changed, and he had to move forward. They were almost to the garage.

Out of the corner of his eye, he could see the older man duck his head. "Yes, you can say that. She was unbelievably kind to my wife when we really needed it."

Jimmy Lee pulled into the garage's parking lot and started once again to apologize. But Pendergast opened the door and jumped down. "Thanks for your own kindness," he said.

The younger man watched Pendergast run through the rain to the office, where he pointed at a dark gray SUV ready to be picked up. Pendergast pulled out his wallet and waved as Jimmy Lee turned to leave.

20

BETHANNE SAT IN HER OFFICE AFTER the Volunteers left, thinking about Sherry saying they hadn't seen Penelope leave, so she must have gone out another door. But that was impossible. Except for the lobby's main door, all the others had key codes. If those door handles were held down for more than fifteen seconds, an alarm sounded and staff came running. No alarm had sounded the day Suzie Cunningham had died.

But if Penelope didn't go out the front door and didn't trigger an alarm with another door, where did she go? Into the empty hallway that connected Skilled Nursing and Assisted Living? Had she hidden in an empty, dark room until a group was leaving the building and joined them? That couldn't work, because that hallway had no view of the front door. She could have crept toward Assisted Living and joined a family group there. Only one person would have signed the group out, and Penelope could have kept in the background, leaving with them.

Bethanne shook her head. Where was all this taking her?

Trudy had come and gone, Charlie's first visitor since he'd moved into Skilled Nursing, and he was feeling a bit tired. All he wanted was lunch, a pain pill and a nap. But that wasn't to be, at least not yet.

Janice Cunningham stuck her head around the door. "Mr. Coleman? I heard about your bad luck, and I had to come visit just as soon as my spa week with the girls was over."

He started to answer, but she bopped in, a vision in tight jeans, high-heeled boots, red sweater and a navy jacket, talking all the while. "I hope you know how totally unique this is." She plunked down in the chair next to his bed. "My first time inside Evergreen's doors." She looked around. "Pretty nice."

The upper half of his bed was raised, so he could see her, unlike when Fred and Willard visited him in the hospital. But he couldn't get a word in edgewise.

Janice leaned over and put a two-pound box of Godiva chocolates on the bed by his soft cast, where he couldn't reach it. "I hope you like these. They're my very favorite."

"Why don't you open it for the both of us," he rushed to get in. "We'll have a little pre-lunch treat."

"Oh, Mr. Coleman, I couldn't possibly," she said. "These're all for you."

"Charlie," he said. "We know each other well enough for you to use my first name." She started to object, but he spoke first, "Come on, get the box open. Maybe we can have two pieces before lunch."

So they sat there and gorged on chocolates while they exchanged news. He told her all about his fall, and she recited everything that had happened from dawn to dark at the Greenbrier Spa.

"Is this really your first time inside Evergreen?" he asked.

"For sure," she said, and a frown grew between her carefully plucked brows. "Rodney came all the time to visit his first wife. He was even here when she died." Janice shook her head like she was clearing a bad vision. Then she positively beamed at Charlie. "But swear to God, I would never have come if it hadn't been for you."

Bethanne, Mae, Eden and Jimmy Lee were all crowded into the back booth at the Corner Cafe. Saturday morning, so lots of folks were there for a late breakfast. The foursome had breakfasted separately long ago. Now they were sitting with coffee and the Cafe's homemade pastries. Outside, it was cold and gusty, a good day to be inside with a hot drink and something sweet. Bethanne had insisted it be her treat, because she was the one to call them together.

Jimmy Lee had previously told Eden what Greg Pendergast said about the help he got for his wife from Suzie Cunningham. Eden had relayed that to Bethanne, who had her own reasons for wanting to pick the brains of the cleverest people she knew.

Bethanne took a bite of her graham cracker pie, contemplated her friends and swallowed. "I know all three of you got better things to do than sit with me on a Saturday morning, but so much has happened that I think we need to share our news." She asked Jimmy Lee to summarize what Pendergast had said, and then she reported what she knew about Rodney and Penelope on the day Suzie Cunningham died.

Happily for Bethanne, Mae didn't need prodding to share her thoughts. "Seems to me we got two mysteries here," her friend said. "Maybe separate, maybe related. Miz Cunningham did something for the Pendergasts. He was practically sneaking in and out of her room. What did she do? And what happened then? Was that somehow a reason for Greg Pendergast to do her in?"

Eden looked like she was ready to agree on the spot as Mae slipped a sliver of butterscotch pie into her mouth and held up a hand signaling she had more to say. "On the other hand, we've got poor Alejandro Garcia saying he saw a woman run out of Miz Cunningham's room just before she died. The Volunteers say her daughter was there, but we don't know where she went. And the staff say Mr. Rodney was definitely there. Can anybody see how those family visits come together?"

Everyone shook their heads, and Mae said, "Me neither." She put down her fork. "For my part, I got a high hurdle to get over. I've known Penelope since she was a little girl. Used to babysit to make a little extra money. Penelope's selfish and self-centered, but it's hard for me to see her doing something to her momma."

Jimmy Lee spoke up. "Could Mrs. Pendergast have been there? Was she the woman Alejandro saw?"

"I don't see how," Bethanne said. "She's been admitted to Memory Care. Kathy Pendergast has trouble navigating almost everywhere. Someone has to come get her and lead her to the dining room, even though it's just down the hall. How could she get in and out of Skilled Nursing without help? And without anyone seeing her?"

Eden was toying with her cherry turnover, pushing bits here and there around her plate. "What if Alejandro was wrong? What if he saw Rodney Cunningham or Greg Pendergast? Hard to get things right when there's a crisis going on."

"Rodney stayed in the room, so Alejandro can't have seen him," Bethanne said. "But Pendergast's not such a big guy. He just might be mistaken for a woman running away in the middle of all that brouhaha."

She was disappointed to see Eden nod her head vigorously at this slim reason for retaining Pendergast on the suspects list. The girl needed to keep a more open mind.

Mae said, "Too late to ask Alejandro to refresh his memory and consider alternative explanations of what he saw." She turned to Bethanne. "When does his sister come back? Would she know anything?"

Bethanne shook her head. "She's on extended leave. There's a rumor she won't be back at all."

Mae nodded. "If we can't find out more about who was running away, we're going to have to keep all options on the table."

Eden tilted her head to the side. "Maybe we need to talk with somebody else." She glanced at Jimmy Lee, who was busy scraping the last of his ice cream brownie off his plate. "Awhile back, Jimmy Lee and I saw Trudy Graham lurking in the garden inside the building that houses Skilled Nursing and Assisted Living. She's awfully snoopy. Maybe she knows something."

Bethanne started nodding and smiling. "It's true. She is snoopy, and she's been asking me questions. Trudy's one of the Volunteers. That means she's ideally placed to learn all kinds of things."

Mae looked around the group and grinned. "So let's invite her to tea."

Meanwhile, Alice and Trudy had finally found time to visit the cemetery and check on Anne-Marie's alibi. On the way, they'd stopped at Blossoms Aplenty, so they could put something in the vase beside Suzie's niche.

As she steered her ancient Chevy sedan through the cemetery gates, Alice was wondering if this effort would pay off. "No way the staff will remember if Anne-Marie were here specifically on the day Suzie died."

Trudy smiled. "Better we find out than just assume what we think we know. At the very least, we'll learn if Anne-Marie makes a regular practice of visiting Tom's grave." Alice made a face, and Trudy added, "Every little bit moves us forward."

"Okay, okay," Alice said. She pulled into the parking lot, and they left the warmth of the car's heater. Winter's cold gusts made Alice wonder if they'd have snow for Christmas. Too far off to know, but it sure felt like a possibility today.

They hurried through the wind to the columbarium, the thick wall housing the urns of the cremated. It was faced with shiny black marble, and Alice could see the reflection of their images, herself lanky and ungainly, Trudy short and round. She noticed herself limping. That happened a lot in cold weather and when she was tired. *Just something I have to manage*, she reminded herself and did her best to keep a normal gait.

When they found Suzie's niche, they took the dead and drooping flowers out of the little, narrow vase, dumped the nasty-smelling water and put in fresh from the nearby tap. Then they added their own arrangement, a fern leaf, a spray of baby's breath and a single red rose.

Trudy took Alice's hand, bowed her head and said, "Lord, we ask your blessing on our sister Susan Cunningham and for our efforts to find out how she truly died. There is so much evil in the world. Please help us root out this little corner of it. Amen."

As Trudy prayed, Alice let her eyes rest on the marble plaque that sealed Suzie's niche. In addition to her birth and death dates, the inscription read:

Susan Bauer Cunningham
Beloved Wife of Rodney
Cherished Mother of Brenda and Penelope

So much said and unsaid there, Alice mused. What would Janice make of "Beloved wife"? And did the list also name a murderer?

As soon as Trudy said, "Amen," Alice pulled her away. "Come on. Let's talk with the staff about Anne-Marie."

They visited the cemetery's main office, the on-site florist (Alice almost sniffed, so poor was the choice of flowers), and the superintendent of grounds. They got the same response everywhere. Yes, Anne-Marie Hull seemed to come to her husband's grave every week, but they thought the day varied. No one could remember that far back, to early September.

"We're going to have to be satisfied with that," Trudy said as she climbed in the car.

Alice nodded, but she wasn't happy about it. She felt like saying, "I told you so," but they'd had enough of that from Willard and Fred.

Those two golf buddies were at it again. They didn't tell the Silver Foxes what they were doing. They simply invited another of Willard's accountant friends for a round of drinks at the Country Club, hoping he would be the spy they needed. It had worked the last time, why not again? Willard was a little dubious about their plan, especially going out on a limb again without talking it over with the group. But Fred was ultimately the stronger personality of the two, and that was that. The man they'd invited was from the firm that did Rodney's books. In fact, he was the one directly in charge of Rodney's account.

The three men were seated in one of the crescent-shaped booths in the wood-panelled bar. The Country Club had been built in the

1920s, when such establishments were mostly for men, and the bar reflected that. Elsewhere, like in the dining room, a less masculine touch had moved the decor into the modern era. But the bar would have fit nicely in any London gentlemen's club of the nineteenth century.

Willard grabbed a handful of peanuts from the table's bowl and squirmed back on the green-leather banquette. "Great being together again, John. Been too long. What's happening in your life these days?"

And with that, his friend was off and running with a narration that covered everything from how his kids were doing in school to his wife's bunion operation, ending with his trials serving clients. That finally provided the opening they needed. Fred had already bought another round of drinks, and the Club's best scotch seemed to be doing the trick as far as loosening up their spy.

"What's happening with Rodney Cunningham's firm?" Willard asked John. "I heard he's developing his wife's old family property."

John swigged his straight scotch and blinked a couple times. "Yeah. He's planning to buy out his daughters' interests in the place, and he's already got the surveyors hard at work."

Willard and Fred never let on they already knew that. "Gonna make a bundle, I bet," Fred said.

John winked. "You betcha."

"Don't know I'd ever have the guts to take on a project like that," Willard said. "Even if I had the money. Rodney ever seem worried to you? Like maybe things might not work out?"

John frowned and scrutinized Willard, who concentrated on getting his last few peanuts into his mouth. John seemed to like what he saw, because he relaxed and finished his scotch. "Oh, Rodney's always stressed. You'd be too if you had his worries to keep you up at night."

"Guess so," Willard said, trying to keep John's suspicions down.

"Hope there's nothing else keeping him awake," Fred said. "Saw him at his first wife's funeral. Did seem upset then, of course."

"And ever since," John said. "Seems like he just hasn't been the same."

Willard worked hard to keep his posture relaxed. "How so?"

John studied his nearly empty glass and raised a who-can-say shoulder. "He's been nervous as a cat ever since the day she died. We had an important meeting the next afternoon, and he couldn't concentrate."

"Only natural," Fred said.

Willard nodded. "Only natural," he repeated. He let a silence grow for a moment and added as if it had just occurred to him. "Couldn't have been anything else, could it?"

"Dunno," John said and sucked the last drop from his glass. "He did say something awful happened at the hospital, and I took it to mean Suzie dying unexpected. But when I got to thinking about it later, it seemed like he was saying it was something connected to her passing."

21

MONDAY MORNING, MAE GLANCED UP when she heard the bobbing bell on the Gifts-n-Such door. Penelope pushed past the shop's wreath with a smile and a wave. "Hi, Miz M," she said, using the pet name she'd called her ever since Mae had been her babysitter.

"Hello, baby girl," Mae said, "You're sure a sight for sore eyes." She came around the counter to give Penelope a big hug, remembering what Alejandro had said and praying he hadn't seen this Cunningham child running away the day her mother died.

Penelope held on just a little longer than seemed necessary, and Mae wondered what was bothering her. Could she be wrong about what'd happened?

Penelope gave a tiny dry cough and said, "I'm way late putting up Christmas decorations in my shop. Whole family down with the flu. I'm just now recovering and trying to catch up." She looked around. "Hope everything's not too picked over."

Mae smiled and led her over to the display. "We've still got some pretty good stuff. See what you like, and I'll give you a discount."

Penelope appeared troubled. "I don't want to take advantage."

Mae shook her head. "You're not. It's getting so close to

Christmas, we were going to put the decorations on sale in a little while. You're a special customer, that's all."

When Penelope had made a selection of Christmas elves and paid, Mae saw her opportunity and took it. "Got time for tea and gingerbread? We'd have to have it here, so I can keep an eye out for customers, but it's been too long since we've been able to visit."

Penelope's smile was weak. "I think I'd like that. Shall I make the tea, so you can stay here?"

"Thanks," Mae said. "You'll find everything you need just through that curtain. Cookies are in a tupperware box." She busied herself moving some items from the counter to a display table, then brought two stools so they could sit where she'd cleared a space.

After a while, Penelope came out with a tray full of napkins, cups, plates and gingerbread women decorated in Christmas colors. She set everything out on the cleared counter-space.

Mae took a long sip of her tea and turned to Penelope. "You doing okay? Been a while since your momma passed, but you're probably going to miss her forever. I know I still miss mine, and it's been years since she left us."

Penelope green eyes turned sorrowful. "Oh, I miss her everyday. I keep thinking I should tell Momma this, or I should tell Momma that. But she's gone, and I'll never be able to tell her anything again."

Penelope's sorrow wrenched Mae's heart, but the older woman knew she had to go on. "Were you able to be with her before she passed? Tell her goodbye? That sure helped me."

"Yeah." Penelope turned red. "I mean no. I wasn't right there when she died, but I did see her that day." She sucked in a long, ragged breath that became a sob and gazed at Mae with what seemed like a longing for what was lost. "Oh, Miz M, we had words. I'll never forgive myself. That was the last we said to each other."

Mae watched Penelope's face. "That'll eat you forever. Do you want to talk about it?"

Penelope's torso shook. "Not now. I'm not ready." She sucked in a breath. "I'm praying to the Lord for his forgiveness, but I have yet to feel it."

Mae nodded. "We know the Lord forgives us if we confess we're truly sorry for what we've done." She looked into Penelope's eyes. "You have to find a way to forgive yourself. I'm here to talk whenever you're ready."

Throughout the whole conversation, Mae had a hard time to contain her own conflicting emotions. When Penelope was a child, she had a way of telling what happened so she'd end up looking innocent, even when she wasn't. Was that what she was doing now? Had Penelope done more than she admitted? If so, what did Mae owe that child? If Penelope did do more, what did Mae owe to justice?

Trudy entered Evergreen's Memory Care facility to visit Greg Pendergast's wife as she'd been doing every morning for a while. She knew it was important to come every day, so she'd become a presence in Kathy Pendergast's life and be remembered. As usual, she signed the guest register and was buzzed in through the secure door. Sadly, all exterior doors in Memory Care had to be kept locked so residents couldn't wander outside and get lost or worse. These doors were also code-keyed and alarmed, just in case.

She walked down the hall, passing a couple residents who were held upright in their wheelchairs by soft restraints, so they wouldn't fall out even if they nodded off. She repressed a shudder. Such a terrible contrast to the active seniors who had apartments in Independent Living. Trudy knew weaker residents had to be secured this way so they could at least be out of their beds and have the minimum stimulation the hallway provided. But it was a dismal scene, nonetheless. She prayed her mind never failed her and then begged God to forgive her for being so self-centered. As she went on, nodding to the staff at the nursing station, she continued her prayer, asking the Lord to watch over all those here who needed help more than she did.

Trudy came to Kathy's room, knocked and entered. As usual, Kathy was dressed, sitting in an easy chair brought from home and looking out at the facility's interior garden. All the leaves were gone from the deciduous trees, but a few holly bushes provided a modicum of color against the brown of winter's grass and the buff brick of the building. Trudy knew not to startle Kathy, so she slowly walked to stand beside the window frame. "Hi, Kathy. How're you doing today?"

Greg's wife turned her head, her face devoid of recognition, her voice hollow. "Hello."

"I'm Trudy. So nice to see you again." Trudy was following guidelines for residents in Memory Care. Remind them of who you are. Don't say, "Remember..."

Kathy gave a wan smile. "Nice to see you." But it didn't seem like she had any recollection of who'd come to visit.

Trudy sat in the visitor's hardback chair and patiently talked with Kathy until it seemed the other woman was remembering her and previous visits. Soon they were laughing over a silly story that Trudy told.

Just then, a male resident wandered in. "Judith? Is that you, Judith?"

Trudy stood, walked over and gently took his arm. "Sorry, I'm afraid you've got the wrong room. Let me take you out to the nursing station, and maybe they can help you." The man came without resisting, and soon Trudy was back in her chair.

Kathy smiled. "Hello, Trudy. Nice to see you again."

"Hello, Kathy. Tell me how you are."

And so it went, until rapport and even some memory had been awakened. Kathy was talking about Greg and how he came everyday to see her. "Such a nice man," Trudy said. "We're both Volunteers in another wing of Evergreen."

"Yes, Evergreen. That's where we are, isn't it?"

Trudy nodded. "I like your room. So pretty, with nice colors and a pretty picture."

"Greg brought that from home. It's my favorite."

"I like it, too. You're lucky to have a husband who cares so much."

"I was mad at him before. When he said I had to come here." Kathy looked around her room. "But it's okay now. People are nice, and Greg doesn't have to worry about me."

"He was worried before?"

Kathy nodded and leaned toward Trudy, lowering her voice. "He had a lot on his mind, but our friend helped."

Trudy felt a jolt of adrenalin, but she tried to keep her posture and voice relaxed and caring. "Your friend?"

"Our friend from church. She gave Greg money so I could come here, and now he doesn't have to worry anymore." Kathy smiled and leaned back. "He comes everyday, and we can have a happy visit."

That same morning, like just about every morning now, Alice was sitting with George in the Evergreen Cafe as they had their coffee and doughnuts. They were reviewing recent events and pondering the way forward. Alice noticed how close together they were, their heads almost touching, close enough she almost brushed his hand in front of hers. She hoped none of the passersby got the wrong idea about what was going on. She also hoped they didn't know what was really going on.

She returned her thoughts to their review. The Silver Foxes had met a couple days ago and exchanged the results of their labors. As expected, Anne-Marie had sworn she'd proven none of the Cunninghams could have done it. But several of the Foxes had said it was too soon to know that for sure. George had related what the homeless man told the Catholic shelter's Sister about being "pretty sure" it was a woman who drove the car that ran Alejandro off the road. Willard and Fred had reported on their fruitless search of body shops. Then they'd tried to brazen it out about getting another accountant drunk, but the two buddies still got seriously admonished for going off on their own yet again.

Trudy was visiting Greg's wife on a regular basis, gaining her trust, and she'd also been invited to tea by Bethanne. The Foxes had tried to puzzle out what, if anything that meant, and agreed that the only way to find out was for Trudy to go drink some tea. Finally Charlie, home from Skilled Nursing and moving around with a cervical collar, soft cast and walker, had described his visit from Janice and how believable she'd been about it being her first time at Evergreen.

When Alice and George got to the end of their review, he scowled. "Still no real resolution on anything."

"But it feels like we're nearly there." Alice grinned. "Like it's just a matter of time."

He smiled back, his face warm with something she couldn't discern. "And then what, O Great Leader? When do we tell Sheriff Price?"

Alice ducked her head with embarrassment at the title he gave her. "Just as soon as we have all the pieces, and they all come together. Not long now, I think."

"Why are you ducking your head?" he asked. "You hide your light under a bushel. Even from yourself." He sat up straight and made a pronouncement. "Alice Dundee, you have a quiet strength and the same sort of leadership. I expect people underestimate you. And so do you."

Alice was spared from answering, because Trudy dashed through the door and over to their table, clearly out of breath.

The grandmother sat down. "I just visited Kathy Pendergast. Poor thing can't remember much, and I want her to know I'm there every day for her."

George spoke up. "Would you like a glass of water? Seems like you ran over here. You must be thirsty."

Trudy adjusted her spectacles, which had slipped down her nose. "Typically thoughtful of you, George. But I want to get this off my chest. Time enough for water later."

"So?" Alice prompted.

"So Suzie gave Greg Pendergast money to pay for his wife's support in Evergreen Memory Care. That entry fee is lots higher than ours was for Independent Living. So's the monthly fee, $7000 per. No wonder Suzie was hard up for money. She was paying her own monthly fee and Kathy Pendergast's too." Trudy shook her head as if in reverence. "Not only that. It would've been just like Suzie to pay Kathy's entry fee plus a full first quarter, all at once."

Alice and George looked at each other and nodded like something had been confirmed. "Can we check that?" Alice asked.

"I don't see how," George said. "That sort of thing is highly confidential. The Director's not going to tell us."

"It all makes sense though," Trudy said. "We know Greg's insurance business is in trouble. He and Suzie acted like very special friends, not only at church but also when she was in Skilled Nursing. Then Suzie was so strapped for cash that she couldn't go out for lunch or shopping with Anne-Marie. Even though they'd been in the habit of doing that."

Alice smiled at George. "Pieces coming together."

He didn't smile back. "But what if Greg Pendergast were a predator? He's at least a decade younger than Suzie, and she'd been without a man in her life for a long time. What if he wormed his way into her affections and hit her up for financial help?"

Trudy's head bobbed. "I was wondering about that too. Giving Suzie the attention she craved, so he could get his hands on her money."

George leaned back and crossed his arms. "Been done before. And it can be awfully hard to prove, especially if the target doesn't want to cooperate. Now Suzie's gone, it's probably impossible to get any proof. Greg can just say it was a gift freely given."

Alice rested her own crossed arms on the table. "Are you thinking that Greg Pendergast would have killed Suzie to keep her gift a secret? Seems pretty far-fetched."

George glanced from one woman to the other. "Like I said, it's been done before. Awfully embarrassing if the whole town found out

Greg was about to go bankrupt and had to borrow money to get his wife the care she needed. He's in the insurance business, for goodness sake. Why didn't he have long-term care policies for them both? And then there's the part about borrowing from his lady-friend. Tongues would wag about what he was giving Suzie in return."

Trudy's forehead creased. "How's Greg going to pay for Kathy's monthly fees now?" She lowered her head and seemed to speak to herself. "Maybe we can set up a fund at church to help out." She raised her eyes to Alice and George. "Some wealthy folk go to that church, some of them philanthropists. I'll look into it."

After Trudy's typically kind thought, Alice hated having to say, "But Greg Pendergast stays a suspect."

"For now," George said.

Trudy shook her head as if to clear it for another subject. "What do I tell Bethanne? I'm supposed to meet her at Gifts-n-Such for tea this afternoon. She's already involved in what might have happened to Suzie, because of what Alejandro said. What if she wants to pick my brain?"

Alice and George looked at each other, exchanging thoughts without talking. "We don't have time to call a meeting of the Silver Foxes before you go over there," she said.

"Trust your instincts," George said. "If Bethanne wants information, she has to give some in return." He started to rise from his chair. "Afraid I've got to take off. Going to get my hearing checked."

"Hearing?" Alice said. "Doesn't seem to me like you're having any trouble."

"Then I'm covering it up pretty good," he said and waved as he turned to go. "Bye, ladies. See you at lunch."

"Now I do need that drink of water," Trudy said to Alice. "Can you hang around for a bit?"

"Sure," Alice said. She watched her friend head for the cold drinks counter, curious to see if Trudy would return with yet another bombshell.

22

Trudy no sooner returned, than Anne-Marie clicked up to their table on her high heels. Alice wondered if she were ever without them. Did she wear those spikes around the house?

"Girls," Anne-Marie gushed, "I'm so excited I just had to tell somebody, and after all we've been through as Silver Foxes, it feels like you're truly my best friends."

She commandeered the chair George had vacated and held onto the edge of the table with both manicured hands, her diamonds shimmering under the Cafe lights. "You'll never believe what I finally got up the nerve to do."

Alice and Trudy gazed at her, speechless and shaking their heads. Surely Anne-Marie hadn't pulled a Fred-and-Willard, going off on her own with the Cunninghams?

"What?" Alice finally got out.

Anne-Marie couldn't contain the smile that stretched her face into a waxy mask. "I've invited George Martino to the Country Club dance on Christmas Eve, and he's accepted!"

Alice carefully kept her own face immobile. Was that why George was getting his hearing checked, so he'd be ready for the big dance?

Anne-Marie was galloping on, clearly unaware of what her new best friends might be thinking. "You probably could tell I was getting interested in George since we've been thrown together so often. Maybe now he's going to get interested in me."

She paused and gave each woman a meaningful look. "I know what, let's all go together and buy ourselves new dresses and shoes for the holidays. You'll need them for Evergreen's New Year's Eve Party, and I'll wear mine to the Country Club." She gave a tiny little frown and dropped her voice, giving the impression she was talking to herself. "No, I need two dresses, one for Christmas Eve and one for New Year's. But the same shoes, maybe silver. Or gold."

Anne-Marie seemed to recollect there were two other people involved. "What do you say? We deserve a treat after everything that's happened since Suzie died."

Alice glanced at Trudy who appeared to be reacting to this monologue the same way she was. "I don't need a new dress," Alice said. "My old green one's good enough."

Trudy started to say something, but Anne-Marie pushed in. "Nonsense. You wear that dress year after year. Makes you look dowdy, it's so out-of-date."

Trudy took back her turn to speak. "Alice could never look dowdy." She paused. "But it's still a good idea to get something new. It'll pep us up."

Alice started shaking her head at Trudy, and the grandmother reached out to pat her arm. "Come on. I need your help deciding, and it'll be fun. We can go to The Boutique. About the only decent place left downtown."

"Nope," said Anne-Marie, "we need something better than that. Let's drive to Harristown. The University Mall has a shop with only dress-up clothes. We'll make a day of it, have lunch at the Riverside Cafe and be home in time for dinner at Evergreen."

"I don't..." Alice started to say, and Trudy interrupted. "I really need you to come." She gave a meaningful movement of her eyeballs toward Anne-Marie. "Help me out now."

Alice finally agreed, but she had no idea how she was going to get through that day.

Their shopping day was still in the future. Today, Trudy had to go to tea with Bethanne. She took a little nap after lunch to be rested. As she drifted off, her visit with Kathy Pendergast played through her waning consciousness and she vowed to continue her visits as long as they both were able to be together. The need to discover what happened between Greg and Suzie was no longer there, but Kathy's greater need not to be forgotten remained.

Trudy woke up creaky. She should have known better. If she stayed active, her PMR improved as the day wore on. If she lay down or sat too long, her joints seemed to freeze up again. "Dummy" she said into the mirror, as she washed her face.

She was soon in her Taurus and driving to Gifts-n-Such. It seemed like a strange place to have tea, but Bethanne had said the holiday season meant tons of customers, so she and Mae both had to work to keep up. When the day was done, Bethanne added, she and Mae often had tea after they closed at five. This was just an expansion of their usual practice.

To her surprise, Trudy found not only Bethanne and Mae waiting for her but also Eden and her young man. Jimmy Lee, that was his name. All these people made Trudy feel uncomfortable, like she was being ambushed. She looked back at the shop door, where

Mae was locking up and turning the "Closed" sign toward the street.

Bethanne seemed to perceive what Trudy was feeling, because she said, "I didn't mean to set you up. It's just that we all need to talk to you. There's a mystery at Evergreen, and we each have a piece of it." She smiled. "You too, I think."

Trudy didn't know what to do. It felt like she shouldn't be here alone. And yet she was.

Charlie had forgotten Trudy was having tea that afternoon at Gifts-n-Such. Lost in his own challenges, he was sitting home watching a track meet on television, bored out of his mind. He'd had way too much sitting around since his accident. And way too much TV. He regarded his walker, positioned within reach beside his chair. *Getting pretty good with that gizmo,* he thought. Good enough to go out on his own? Only one way to find out.

He raised his recliner into the upright position, feeling safe about the next maneuver. They'd put a kind of orthopedic boot on his left leg, so it was possible to get around with a walker. He pulled it around and used it to stand. Just like he'd been taught in rehab, and he did it smoothly, if he said so himself.

Charlie leaned on the walker, but not as much as had been necessary only a couple days before. That felt good. Then he got himself to the coat closet. Putting on his jacket and cap made him feel even better, and it was so much simpler now the cervical collar was off. He already had a thick-soled sneaker on his right foot, so he was good to go.

Out the door and down the hall, through the glass entrance and just stand there, breathing in the fresh air. A smile spread across Charlie's face, as he felt his lungs fill for the first time in days. Nobody around, thank goodness. He didn't need any overly solicitous helpers trying to get him back inside.

Now what? Maybe a little tour around the parking lot, flat and easy to navigate. The weak sunshine felt good on his face, and he stopped to enjoy the sensation, eyes shut and head turned upward. He felt as much as heard the car pull in front of him. Darn. Who was it? Was this going to ruin his little adventure?

"Hi, Mr.......Charlie."

He knew that voice. Charlie opened his eyes and peeped through the open driver's window at blond-streaked waves falling onto the shoulders of a purple track suit. Janice Cunningham in her champagne Lexus.

"I was running at the track," she said. "That made me think of you, so I came by to see if you'd like to go for a ride." Her right eye fluttered in a wink. "Active man like you needs to get out now and then."

"Oh boy, would I," Charlie said. "Let's go downtown and have us some pie."

Didn't take long for Janice to help him into the passenger seat, stow his walker and hit the road to the Corner Cafe.

Across the street from the Cafe, Bethanne was escorting Trudy to one of the chairs around a tea table in full view of the shop window.

Well, thank goodness for that, Trudy thought. Truth to tell, she wasn't sure what was going on, so she felt reassured to be in sight of passersby.

Mae and the kids had disappeared into the back room, but it was only moments before they returned with trays of everything they needed for a Christmas tea. Two steaming pots, one smelling like

Lady Grey, the other like mint. A plate piled with decorated sugar cookies in every shape of the season, another covered in individual mince pies, a dollop of hard sauce on top of each one.

Bethanne grinned. "No way I made any of this. Mae's the baker." She helped unload the two cozy-covered pots. "I did start the tea though."

Eden passed around paper plates with a holly motif and napkins to match. Jimmy Lee distributed plastic forks and spoons, while Mae made sure all the goodies were within reach. "Help yourself, Miz Graham," the large woman said. "Please don't stand on ceremony. You're among friends."

Trudy's face must have shown what she was thinking about that, because Bethanne said, "We want to exchange information about Miz Cunningham's death."

Wow, Trudy thought. *I need the Silver Foxes here. Or at least Alice and George.* She tried very hard to keep any inkling of those thoughts to herself.

"Let me start," Bethanne continued, "We're going to tell you everything we know, so you can be sure we're not playing games." She reviewed who was visiting around the time Suzie died.

Trudy nibbled on a cookie, drank some tea and waited. She'd heard all this from Bethanne before, except for the part about Rodney and the pillow. That news caused her nibble to bounce halfway down, a token of her discomfort at being the only Silver Fox present. It wasn't that she didn't feel safe. More that she didn't want to make the same mistakes George and Fred and Willard had made when they were off on their own.

Mae shifted in her chair, like she was searching for a more

comfortable position. "That's just by way of summary," she said and looked anxious.

What was coming? Trudy wondered. Would she have to pay tit for tat, telling what she knew?

"I've had to give this a lot of thought," Mae continued. "Didn't even tell my friends here until I asked the Lord what to do. I had to feel positive it was right, breaking the confidence of someone I've known since she was a little girl."

Oh dear, Trudy thought, *what little girl?*

Mae shifted her bulk again and bit her lips before speaking. "Penelope Cunningham had words with her mother the day she died. I know because she told me, and I've been troubled ever since. What if she got Miz Cunningham so upset, it killed her?"

"We know Miz Cunningham was in Skilled Nursing because she had heart palpitations," Bethanne said. "She was having anxiety attacks, and the doctor prescribed propranolol. She seemed to be doing better. Almost ready to go home, but a fight with her daughter could've overloaded her with stress and..." Bethanne's voice trailed off.

Eden spoke up, "But what about that pillow? Did Rodney Cunningham use it to smother his wife?"

"Come on now," Jimmy Lee said. "Feels like you're jumping to conclusions again."

Eden made a face at him. "Okay, but you gotta admit it's a possibility." She tilted her head like another idea had come to her. "Or maybe his daughter did it. Had an argument and lost control."

Trudy was having trouble taking it all in. Meanwhile, Mae was shaking her head like she couldn't agree.

Jimmy Lee smiled at Eden, but it didn't seem friendly to Trudy, more like patronizing. "Whatever happened to your suspicions of Greg Pendergast?" he said.

Eden crossed her arms and nodded like a sage on TV. "Could've been any of them."

Trudy found it hard to swallow. The sugar cookie had turned to dust. The tea was going down the wrong way. So much to take in. What in the name of God should she do now?

23

Janice was going on about her recent shopping trip to Pittsburgh, getting ready for the holidays. New dress for this, new shoes for that. A completely new outfit for the Cunningham's annual Open House. "Do you think you could come, Charlie?"

He took the last bite of his chocolate cream pie and glanced out the window. There was Trudy, sitting just inside the window of Gifts-n-Such with a whole gang of folks. And she was choking. At least it seemed like it. That large African-American woman who owned the shop with Bethanne was pounding Trudy on the back, and the girl who ran the EverTeens was holding out a glass of water. Bethanne and the young guy looked as distressed as everyone else seemed to be.

"Charlie?" Janice said, "Could you come to our Open House? It's on the eighteenth."

"What? Oh, too soon to tell." He reached for his walker. "Janice, could you help me get across the street? Looks like a friend of mine is in trouble."

By the time they got to the shop, things inside seemed to have calmed down. Charlie banged on the door. Trudy glanced their way and motioned for someone to let them in. Bethanne opened the door, and Trudy said, "I'm more embarrassed than anything. But I'm awfully glad to see you."

Charlie leaned on his walker and watched the action, trying to figure out what was going on. Trudy glanced at Janice, standing beside Charlie. Then she turned to the Gifts-n-Such group. "I think you can see what you've told me has been upsetting." She gazed at Bethanne. "I need to talk with some folks who are looking into similar questions. I can say that you're right, we probably know some things you don't, but these are not my facts to tell without consulting my friends."

She raised her eyebrows at Charlie, and he was happy to nod his approval. "Once I do that," Trudy continued, "I promise to get back to you. Maybe we all need to meet together."

Bethanne and Mae gazed at each other and seemed to come to an understanding. But before they could speak, Eden said, "That meeting has to include Jimmy Lee and me. We got a stake in this too." The young man bobbed his head in agreement.

It seemed to Charlie like she was going to say more, but Bethanne interrupted, speaking to Trudy. "You talk over a meeting with your friends, and all four of us..." She gave the EverTeen leader a positive look. "...will be standing by for a date and hour that works for everyone."

Charlie figured it was time to go and put a hand on Trudy's shoulder. "You feeling good enough to drive?"

She smiled. "Yeah. Just choked for a minute. But I'm all right now. Let's go home and talk to Alice."

He and Janice walked Trudy to her Taurus. Slowly, because of his orthopedic boot and walker, but Charlie reflected maybe the pace was good for Trudy too. "We'll drive behind, just in case," he said, and Trudy inclined her head like she was grateful.

Once Charlie and Janice were back in her Lexus, she said, "What was that all about? Looked like a bunch of secrets to me."

Charlie chose his words carefully. "Probably just a lot of hokum. You know how folks can get all worked up over nothing."

Janice gave him a funny look, but she dropped the subject.

When they got back to Evergreen, Trudy listened as Charlie kept the lid on Janice's curiosity, not knowing it was the second time he'd made the effort. Then Trudy and Charlie headed for Alice's apartment. It was slow going. He seemed tired, and she was concerned for him. Trudy was also interested in why he was at the Corner Cafe with Janice, but this wasn't the time to ask.

Charlie may have been tired and focused on getting to Alice's apartment, but not so much he couldn't speak. "What the heck happened at the shop?"

Trudy gave him a quick overview, and they agreed that they had to run it by Alice and organize a meeting with the Silver Foxes as soon as possible. But when they got to her door and repeatedly rang her bell, they had to accept that Alice wasn't there.

Trudy observed Charlie. He was plainly starting to fade, slumped over his walker and breathing too hard. "Okay," she said, "Alice isn't home. Let's get you back to your apartment. We'll both take a little rest and meet everyone for dinner as usual."

Charlie answered like he was peevish from fatigue. "That's not going to work, and you know it. We can't talk about something like that in the dining room."

"No," Trudy said, "but we can say enough to convince everyone we have to meet just as soon as we can."

"Okay, okay," he said and began to turn toward his apartment.

Even though Trudy knew he'd practiced this maneuver scores of time in rehab, he seemed to get tangled up in the walker. He stumbled, and she put out a hand to steady him.

He started to shake her off, but she kept her hand where it was and said, "Remember last year? Before I finally got my PMR diagnosed? You never failed to help when I was crippled with pain. Now you've got to let me have my turn. Fair is fair."

Charlie stopped and gazed at her, his face full of changing emotions that were hard to decipher. Finally, he said, "You're right. We do help each other, and it's your turn now."

The Silver Foxes had been at their usual dinner table for some time when Trudy and Charlie arrived. Alice watched Trudy help him get settled and put his walker in an alcove where other residents had stashed theirs out of the way.

"Something happened this afternoon that we need to discuss as soon as possible," Charlie said. "You tell them, Trudy."

She sat down. "You all know I went to tea this afternoon. I don't want to name names, but there were four people there, and I heard the most remarkable story about what happened the day our friend died."

Fred threw his head back, crossed his arms and squinted down his nose at Trudy. "So of course, you told them everything we know. Couldn't hold back, could you?"

Charlie almost snarled and started to answer. Alice felt the need to intervene, but Trudy spoke for herself. "No. I said I needed to talk with you all and I'd get back to them about a joint meeting if we thought it was the right thing to do."

Fred brought his chin down level. "Well, that's something, I guess."

"That's enough," Alice said. "Can everyone come to my apartment after dinner, and we'll talk tonight?" When all heads dipped in agreement, she said, "Good. Now let's change the subject until we can be alone."

"Good idea," George said. "Will everybody be here for the holidays?"

"So many fun events to look forward to," Anne-Marie said with a meaningful look at George, but he turned to Trudy. "Tell us about Evergreen's plans for Christmas. Lots of wonderful decorations?"

Fred glanced at Charlie. "Don't fall off the ladder again."

Alice wasn't surprised at the Foxes' predictable responses when Trudy later reported on her teatime conversation. Everyone was flabbergasted to learn Penelope could be a suspect, but then each Fox had their own take on what they'd heard.

"That twinkie?" asked Fred, clearly not ready to believe she could have killed her mother.

He was backed up by Anne-Marie for different reasons. "I refuse to believe that any Cunningham could have murdered Suzie. No reason for anyone to do that." She scanned the group, her eyes lingering on George. "Just because they had words. Who doesn't have words now and then? But we don't kill over it."

"Fifty bucks says it was about money," Willard said. "Penelope hitting her mother up for cash and being told there wasn't any to be had."

George urged everyone to keep an open mind until they had all the facts.

Alice was tired of all this hashing the same things over and over. "So how soon do we want to meet with Bethanne and her friends?" she asked.

"Hold on," Fred said. "Who says we want to?"

"I do," Willard responded, and almost everyone agreed.

But not Fred, who crossed his arms and looked glum.

Anne-Marie spoke up. "I refuse to be a part of this. I will not be disloyal to my friends."

"We're not being disloyal," George said, "We're trying to gather facts about what happened when Suzie died."

To Alice's surprise, Anne-Marie declined to be placated, even though it was George who made the effort.

In the end, everyone except Anne-Marie agreed to meet, and they came up with a couple dates that would work for all. Trudy was asked to relay those dates, and everyone went home to bed.

After everybody had gone, Alice let Chow-Fan out. The Siamese proceeded to give Alice a piece of her mind in her loudest, most piercing voice. Alice picked her up, sat on the couch and soothed her with cheek rubs. That always did the trick. Meanwhile, she thought about Anne-Marie. What was going on? Was she a suspect, despite what they'd learned at the cemetery? True, she and Trudy hadn't learned definitively that Anne-Marie had been visiting her husband's grave when Suzie died, but it sure seemed likely. Still, her refusal to accept the guilt of any Cunningham was perplexing.

24

TRUDY PHONED ALICE THE NEXT MORNING with good news. Bethanne had got back in touch almost immediately and said the second date would work best for her group.

"That leaves a couple days to fill," Trudy said. "If we have to wait, let's go shopping with Anne-Marie."

"I really don't think..." Alice began, but Trudy wouldn't let her finish. "Shopping with Anne-Marie would heal any bad feelings left over from last night's meeting. Besides, you and I could both do with something new, and I really and truly don't want to go without you."

Alice considered that the shopping trip might be a chance to look into an explanation of Anne-Marie's puzzling behavior. So she told Trudy she'd go and then called Evergreen's Social Director to reserve the Game Room for a meeting of both groups. At 5:30, so everyone, including working people and high school students, would be free to attend. Next, she phoned Anne-Marie. To her surprise, the other woman seemed to harbor no hard feelings and volunteered to drive to Harristown the following day.

Alice stood before the three-way mirror in Grace's Dress Shoppe at the University Mall, looking at the silvery dress and wondering whatever possessed her to even try it on. The mirror was in a common space with dressing rooms tucked around, and it wasn't long before Trudy and Anne-Marie joined her.

"That's it!" Anne-Marie enthused. "Positively your dress. Goes with your coloring, makes you look younger and definitely in style."

Alice shot a look for help at Trudy, but her friend didn't seem to get the message.

"You look lovely in that dress," Trudy said. "You like long sleeves, and those flare down to the wrist. You never wear a short skirt, and this one comes mid-calf. The whole thing fits nicely, not too tight and not too loose." She gave Alice her sweetest smile. "I do hope you'll get it."

Alice started to demur, and Trudy rushed on. "It'll make me feel better about getting this one for myself. What do you think?"

Trudy turned slowly, and Alice surveyed her blue silk dress, wondering what to say. She'd never cared much about clothes, only shopping when she needed something and not paying attention to style. But something about this dress... "You look like somebody going to a holiday party," Alice said. "Festive and well, belle of the ball."

Anne-Marie added, "Positively the right dress for you. You're on the committee, and you want to stand out."

"I don't know about that," Trudy said. "But I do like the style. Let's face it, I'm a little plump, and having the belt up under the bust helps disguise my tummy."

"I know what you mean about tummies," Anne-Marie said. "Thank goodness I brought some Spanx to try on dresses. Otherwise, I'd never get into this gold lamé. What do you think? How does it look?"

Alice and Trudy watched as Anne-Marie twisted this way and that in front of the three-way mirror.

Trudy seemed to struggle for something to say. "Goes with your hair."

"Will you be able to sit?" Alice asked.

Later, at the Riverside Cafe, the three chose from the gourmet menu with enthusiasm. Evergreen's food was good, but this was really special. Alice ordered veal marsala, while Trudy selected chicken cordon bleu, and even Anne-Marie forsook her usual Cobb salad for filet mignon with a side of marinated mushrooms and fennel.

"I'm so glad I found two dresses," Anne-Marie said. "One for New Year's at the Evergreen and another for the Club's Christmas Eve dinner-dance." The crinkles around her eyes deepened, and she smiled. "Must look my best for George."

Alice felt Trudy looking at her, but she pretended to be deeply engrossed in her veal.

Shoes next," Anne-Marie said as she cut a tiny slice of mignon. "I'm going for gold all the way. Gold sandals and a bag to match. They'll finish off the outfit to perfection. I already have black peau de soie for the teal-colored dress." She looked at her companions and batted her lashes like one of them was George. "The color of that dress is a perfect match for my eyes."

Alice found herself feeling sorry for Anne-Marie, trying to be the merry widow, probably insecure and lost without a husband. The mood overwhelmed any desire Alice had to pursue Anne-Marie's odd behavior about the Cunningham's possible guilt. At least for now.

To Alice's bewilderment, Anne-Marie came to the joint meeting of the Foxes and Bethanne's group. But then, Alice reflected, George was there, so maybe that had swung Anne-Marie's decision.

Alice and Trudy had talked over the logistics in advance and decided it was important to organize things so both groups had the sense of being equal, especially because they were meeting on the Silver Foxes' turf. That decision resulted in arranging the Game Room chairs in a circle, with Alice and Bethanne sitting side-by-side.

Alice began by thanking everyone for coming, being especially careful to include Anne-Marie in her glance. The widow was sitting next to George, so she probably already felt good about being there.

"Let's start with introductions," Alice said. "We call ourselves the Silver Foxes, because that's how we feel, gray-haired but still bright-eyed and bushy-tailed. My name is Alice Dundee, and I'm a retired professor of math and computer science." She couldn't help but notice Bethanne's young friend, Eden, perk up at the mention of her former profession. Then she realized she'd probably left out the most important fact. "We're all friends of Suzie Cunningham," Alice said, "and we're suspicious that her death wasn't from natural causes."

Heads nodded around the circle, including Bethanne's and her friends'. Alice gestured at Bethanne. "I think most of us know about all the wonderful work you do with our Volunteers, but why don't you say a few words about yourself, and we'll go around the circle until everyone has a turn."

When they'd all finished, Alice felt like they had a fighting chance of remembering each other's information and maybe their names too. "Bethanne," she said, "would you like to start with what you all know, or would you like to hear what we've learned?'

Bethanne consulted her team, and they all agreed they'd like to hear from the Silver Foxes first. So they took turns reviewing everything they'd discovered.

When Trudy talked about Suzie lending Greg Pendergast the money for his wife to be in Evergreen's Memory Care, Eden butted in. "I told you," she said, her voice full of triumph. "I knew there was more to it. I saw it. I saw how he treated her, like a golden bank. Now we know why."

Jimmy Lee held up a hand toward Eden. "Hold on. Let's hear what everyone has to say. Don't wanna jump to conclusions before we have all the facts." Eden squirmed some under that hand, but she also nodded just the slightest bit.

Alice watched this exchange and thought about what it might mean. Jimmy Lee talked like a country boy, but Eden's speech slipped now and then between the Queen's English and something a little country too. Was Eden pulling away from her less-educated friend?

"I think those are our main points," Alice said and turned to Bethanne. "Your turn."

Bethanne reviewed what everyone already knew about Alejandro and who visited Suzie just before she died, as well as what the nurse saw.

"Dammit!" Fred exclaimed. "Let's cut to the chase."

Alice sighed and focused one of her classroom looks on him, the one she used when students got unruly. "Once we've heard everything there is to hear, we can talk about what it means. Until then, Bethanne has the floor."

Bethanne turned to Mae, who sat there with her head down, clearly feeling uncomfortable. Alice watched the large woman struggle with what seemed like personal torment. Mae shuffled her feet as if wanting them to take her away before she had to speak. Finally she took a deep breath and told about her conversation with Penelope.

"Absolutely impossible," Anne-Marie said. "Hasn't that darling girl suffered enough?"

George broke in before she could go on. "Aren't we getting close to the time that we need to go to Sheriff Price with what we know?'

Eden stood up, hands on hips. "We have to solve this mystery ourselves, just like we did before. We got three suspects, but I know Pendergast did Miz Suzie in, and I'm going to prove it."

Fred stood too. "I'm with Eden. Let's catch that sucker." Eden started to smirk, but then Fred added. "But it's not Pendergast. It's Rodney for sure. Smothered his wife with a pillow, then dropped it like a hot potato." He looked triumphant. "I knew he did it from the start."

Eden sat down, looking sullen and bad-tempered.

Willard reached up to pull Fred back in his seat. "You don't know that, and neither do we. Where's the proof?"

Fred jerked his arm away. "I'll get it. You'll see." Despite his upset, he took his seat.

Bethanne directed her attention to Mae. Her friend, normally so tranquil, seemed ready to pop. "What about Penelope?" Bethanne asked.

Mae held onto the seat of her chair with both hands. "I don't want to get Penelope in trouble if we don't have to."

"Listen to us," Alice said. "We're all over the place. Isn't it time to let the Sheriff take charge?"

"Over my dead body," Fred said.

Charlie smiled at Fred. "I'm invited to the Cunningham's holiday Open House. That's this Friday. Maybe I can learn something there."

"Take me with you," Fred said. "I'll beard the lion in his den."

Charlie shook his head. "What? Take you as my date? No way. I was thinking of inviting Trudy." He contemplated the woman beside him. "Two heads are better than one."

Trudy smiled at him and nodded, looking positively delighted.

Anne-Marie spoke up. I'll be there too, but I refuse to be a party to this."

Willard's grin was like a possum's. "Nobody's asking you to."

George smiled at Anne-Marie, his voice conciliatory. "All you need do is have a good time at one of the season's best festivities and forget about anything else. Can you do that?"

Anne-Marie clenched her hands. "I hate this. Being at the Cunninghams and knowing Charlie and Trudy will be snooping."

Alice saw chagrin creep up Trudy's face, while Charlie seemed ready to take umbrage.

Anne-Marie rushed ahead. "It feels like I'll be betraying my friends."

George gave her a gentle reminder. "Suzie was your friend too."

Bethanne changed the subject. "I agree with Alice and George. There's nothing more we can do. Or should do. Time to let the professionals do their job."

"I hear what you're saying," Jimmy Lee said, "but I hear the others too. We got some loose ends here and there. Maybe we should take a few days and see what else we can find out. After that, we go to Jerry Price with whatever we got. I learned my lesson with him when Miz Simmons was killed. Don't take too long telling what you know. But he don't wanna be bothered with small potatoes neither."

In the end, it was agreed that Charlie and Trudy should go to the Cunningham's party and see what more, if anything, they could discover about Rodney. Anne-Marie held her tightly clasped hands in her lap and stared at the wall, refusing to having anything to do with that decision. Mae hung her head but agreed to talk with Penelope one more time to see if she could learn more about her argument with Suzie.

Bethanne turned to George. "Is Brenda out as a suspect for sure?"

"Very likely," he said.

"For sure!" Anne-Marie corrected.

Alice raised her eyebrows to both indicating the need for discretion, and they gave minute nods back. Alice glanced around the group, but to her relief, no one seemed to notice those nods.

"Okay," Eden said, "But what about Greg Pendergast?" She grinned. "I'll get back on his case."

"No, you won't," Jimmy Lee said. "We already heard Miz Trudy has an in with him at church and with his wife in Memory Care. She's the best one to follow up about whether or not Pendergast is a predator."

Alice looked around the group. Eden was positively sulking. Trudy looked unhappy but willing to follow through with Greg Pendergast, and Mae seemed like she'd rather do anything than talk to Penelope.

25

TRUDY CALLED ALICE AFTER THE MEETING. They spent some time reviewing what had happened, and then Trudy put her secret plan into action. "The Cunningham's party is tomorrow. I'm going to get my hair done, and I'm treating you to the same." She heard Alice draw breath to object and delivered her coup de grâce. "Already made the appointments for Friday morning. This is your Christmas present from me, so you really can't say no."

While Trudy was talking with Alice, Charlie was phoning Janice Cunningham. "Sorry to be so late replying to your kind invitation," he said. "I wanted to be sure I'd recovered enough not to be a bother."

"Oh, you could never be a bother, Charlie," she said. "I really love how you listen to me, even when what I'm talking about can't be that interesting. You make me feel like I matter." She sniffled, and Charlie wondered if she was getting soppy on him, but then she went on. "We always have our Open House first thing in the season. That way, we get everyone before they're worn out, and it's always so lively." She seemed to realize maybe she'd said the wrong thing. "But if you get too tired, you can always sit down. So you'll come, right?"

"I'd sure like to." He paused. "Would you mind if I bring my lady-friend?"

"The one I met the other day? At Gifts-n-Such?"

"One and the same," Charlie said.

"Oh gosh, yeah. I'd love to get to know her. I bet she's just as special as you are."

"She's a lot better'n I am," Charlie said.

Trudy drove Alice to her downtown hair salon Friday morning. A hairdresser came to Evergreen once a week. Trudy knew that was where Alice always got hers cut, preferring to do everything else herself until it was time for the next trim. But Trudy was determined. Alice was going to get a new style, and Trudy would never have to look at that shaggy head again.

The two women went in the dressing room, changed into short, black kimonos to cover their torsos and returned to the salon. Alice seemed shellshocked already. "You first," Trudy said to her friend. "This is Tammy, the best stylist in the county, and I can't wait to see what she does with your mop." She smiled to take the sting out of her last words.

Trudy sat in a nearby chair, grinning as Tammy trimmed the mop into a short bob and blow-dried it to perfection.

"I'll never be able to do that myself," Alice said.

"You don't have to," Tammy said. "I cut it so it'll look nice air-dried too. I just wanted you to see how it might look for a festive occasion."

Alice looked bewildered, and Trudy said, "Give it a try. What've you got to lose? You can always go back to your old style if you can't keep this up."

Tammy held up a tall plastic bottle. "I recommend that you use this shampoo once a month." She opened the cap and showed Alice what was inside.

"It's purple," Alice exclaimed, "My hair's not purple."

Trudy spoke up, "Neither is mine. But we ladies with gray hair need to be careful it doesn't go all brassy on us." Alice started to shake her head. "Take the shampoo," Trudy said. "It's part of your Christmas present."

Alice appeared too weary to argue.

Meanwhile, Bethanne was minding the store at Gifts-n-Such. That freed up Mae to have coffee with Penelope behind the closed curtain at the back. Bethanne was careful to stay near the front of the store, so Penelope would feel free to confide.

Mae had had to dig deep to find the fortitude to learn more about what happened between Penelope and her mother. She'd spent a lot of time on her knees since the meeting in the Evergreen Game Room. She'd talked it over with Big Jim. And with Bethanne. Finally she'd decided she had to go ahead, but she was still miserable about it.

But once the decision was taken, she got on with it, just as she'd done with so many challenges in life, from Big Jim losing fingers in an accident to her daughter's pregnancy with a guy who took off as soon as he heard about it.

Mae passed Penelope's favorite, snickerdoodles, asking about her family and her artificial flower business. The younger women was happy to report that all was well at home, and Christmas always brought in customers who didn't want to be bothered with the real thing, whether it was wreaths or boughs of holly.

When Mae felt like she'd established the right atmosphere for sharing confidences, she said, "I've had you on my mind ever since you told me you had words with your Momma the day she died. I'm praying for you, hoping everything's going to be all right."

Penelope literally wrung her hands. "I don't know that it ever will be."

"Remember what the Bible says. "The Lord heals the brokenhearted and binds up our wounds.""

"Not my wounds," Penelope said. "Not the ones I caused either." She drew in a long, shuddering breath and spoke so low Mae almost couldn't hear. "I killed Momma."

Mae felt doubled over, like Penelope had punched her in the stomach. "What do you mean? Your Momma died of a heart attack."

"Yes, but I caused it." Tears made tracks down Penelope's cheeks. "I knew she was doing without herself so she could give money to Greg Pendergast to help his wife. So I came up with a plan to turn Great Oaks into a B&B." She nodded her head from side to side. "I admit part of the attraction was a new project for me, but it also meant money for Momma. I wanted to give her half the income, so maybe she could go back to the kind of life she'd always had."

Mae reached out to put her queen-sized hand on Penelope's thin arm, trying to give her the courage to go on.

"Oh, Miz M," Penelope's voice was a wail, but low enough it couldn't carry beyond the curtain. "That was all wrong. Momma was so mad at me, she spit out her words in a whisper. No one could hear but me. She said strangers would never sleep in the house that had nurtured generations of our family. That house was for my kids and Brenda's kids and children yet unborn. 'How could you be so callous?' she said, 'How could I have raised a daughter so unfeeling?'"

Penelope's nose was running, and she wiped it with a Christmas napkin. She put a shaky hand up to blotchy cheeks. "That's when Daddy arrived, just when it seemed like Momma was choking. She put a hand to her chest, and she couldn't get a breath. I was terrified. Daddy hit the call button and told me to get away quick."

Mae hated herself for having to ask. "Was anybody else there?"

Penelope seemed flustered. "In the room? No. Just Daddy and me."

"And nobody else around to see what was happening?"

Penelope made a face. "That flower man was in the hall. Looked at me like I was a banshee."

Mae sat there, feeling conflicted. Should she believe Penelope? Or was the young woman playing the same game she used to play as a little girl, getting people on her side before all the facts came out? After Penelope scurried out of the shop with her head down, Bethanne asked what had happened. Mae said, "I need to pray over this first. Then I promise we'll talk."

That evening, Trudy drove Charlie to the Cunningham's and left the car with the valet to park. Trudy noticed that Charlie was stronger. He was off the walker and managing quite well with a cane. She wondered if it helped that the cane was passed down from his grandfather, the handle beautifully carved into a duck's head. Even with one pant leg rolled up to accommodate his soft cast, he still looked distinguished in his dark suit and a tie striped in red-and-green.

They passed shrubbery draped in tiny winkling lights and lantern poles wrapped in red and white like candy canes. At the top of each pole, just below the modern globe, was a huge green bow.

Janice met them at the door in a short, stretchy, red velour dress and shoes to match with red ribbons that criss-crossed up her legs from ankle to knee. Trudy considered the green velvet she'd worn to the last New Year's party and felt glad she'd worn it again. The long skirt hid her legs. They couldn't have compared with Janice's even when Trudy was twenty. It didn't help that a diamond-and-ruby pendant swung from Janice's enormous bust. Then Trudy's sense of humor took over, and she almost laughed at her own silliness.

"Come in, come in!" Janice exclaimed, her voice just a tad too bright. She tilted a half-empty champagne flute in her left hand and held out her right to Trudy. "So glad to see you! You're Charlie's special friend." She winked at him. "I've been dying to talk with you ever since we saved you at Gifts-n-Such."

Trudy was a little disconcerted. Where was that remark leading? She looked at Charlie, and he offered a comforting nod, but her concern remained.

The three entered the two-story foyer of Lewiston's most modern mansion, walls nearly all glass and angles going off in multiple directions. The scent of conifers was so heavy, Trudy felt like her head was suspended over the humidifier the doctor had prescribed last winter when her chest was congested. Pine boughs were draped with red ribbons along the bannister of glass panels set in black metal posts. More of the same adorned the super-modern chandelier with glass globes sticking out every which way. The floor-to-ceiling bay window held a twenty-foot Christmas tree laden with all manner of decorations from tiny toys to crystal balls, large and small.

"Where's Rodney?" Charlie asked, and Janice seemed to shrink ever so little.

"Oh, he's around here somewhere," she said. "Probably at the bar with his buddies."

A maid with a sprig of holly pinned to her black dress came forward. "May I take your coats?"

"Not before I get Charlie under the mistletoe," Janice declared and pointed to the ball of tiny green leaves and tinier white berries intertwined with red ribbon and suspended from the chandelier. She planted a kiss on his cheek and smiled at Trudy. "I know you won't mind. Charlie's the uncle I never had."

Trudy didn't mind at all. Whatever it took to get Janice to open up.

Rodney's wife fluttered her fingers and headed back to the guests waiting at the door. "Time to mingle. Catch you two later."

Relieved of their coats, Trudy and Charlie dutifully mingled, greeting a number of old friends and catching up on their news. The buffet was lavish, tiny cream puffs filled with lobster, meatballs on candy-cane-colored toothpicks, Melba toast with sour cream and caviar, glasses of champagne that seemed to stretch to infinity, as well as a bar apparently stocked with every liquor known to humanity. There seemed no end to the temptations, and the two helped themselves to enough for dinner, knowing Evergreen's evening meal would be over by the time they got back.

They found a couple chairs beside a small table and sat down. "All this fancy food must've been ordered online," Trudy said. "Nobody around here caters like this." Charlie sipped his champagne. "Guess Rodney's not hurting for money, even if he can't sell those lots yet."

"Shhhh," Trudy said. "Not the time or place to say that."

He hung his head but still looked at her with mischief in his eyes. "Okay." He raised his chin to signal toward Rodney, who was across the room with an adoring audience of women, each with champagne flute in hand. "That must be one fascinating story," Charlie said, a grin erupting on his lips.

Behind them, Trudy could see Anne-Marie in earnest conversation with Brenda, who then gestured toward a closed door, and led their fellow Fox out of the room. *Uh-oh*, Trudy thought, *do we need to worry about that?*

Just then Janice came up with three new flutes of champagne. She handed two of them over and helped Charlie to his feet, nearly spilling his and her drinks. "Come on," she said. "Let's have us a chat." She opened the door to a darkened family room. Trudy thought about Brenda doing the same thing with Anne-Marie, maybe a different room but another private conversation. Janice turned the rheostat so the lights came up just enough to brighten their way and sat them down on banquettes upholstered in red leather. Charlie let out a sigh, and Trudy wondered if he was in pain.

Janice grinned at him. "Time to tell me about those secrets."

"What secrets?" Charlie said, but even Trudy could tell he was bluffing.

"Them secrets you two was going home to tell Alice." Janice seemed to catch herself, as if realizing her language was giving her roots away. Even at a distance of five feet, Trudy could smell the champagne fumes. They radiated not just from her glass, but from Janice's whole body.

"You know what I mean," Janice said, listing toward Charlie, "the ones you tried to pass off as hokum." She crossed her legs and almost fell off the edge of the banquette. "Who's Alice, anyway?"

"Oh, nobody..." Charlie started to say, but Trudy realized it wouldn't work.

"A friend," she said. "One of the Silver Foxes." She saw Janice's eyebrows go up. "We all knew Suzie Cunningham, and we don't think she died of natural causes."

"Well, of course, she didn't," Janice said.

26

ALICE GLANCED AROUND THE TABLE for four. With Trudy and Charlie at the Cunninghams' party along with Anne-Marie, she found herself surrounded by men tucking into Evergreen's swiss steak and mashed potatoes with abandon. Meanwhile, she picked at her green beans and wondered what was going on at the Open House.

"Something bothering you?" George asked with a kindly smile. "I can feel those wheels turning."

Willard and Fred looked up from their plates, and Alice tried to sound casual. "Just thinking about Trudy and Charlie."

"Should've been me went with Charlie," Fred said.

"You're a bull in a china shop," Willard said. "Trudy can find out stuff because she knows not to come on too strong."

Fred grinned and cupped a hand behind his ear. "Can't hear you."

"Turn up your damn hearing aid then," Willard replied.

Fred put on his smug face. "If Trudy finds out anything, she'll find out Rodney killed Suzie. Just like I said all along."

Alice felt like all she did was admonish people to be careful about what they said in public. "We don't want to be talking like that here."

"Alice is right," George said. "Let's change the subject."

Fred smirked like a child determined to be naughty. "What do you suppose Mae found out from Penelope?"

In the Cunningham family room, Trudy was treading lightly. "Gosh," she said to Janice while trying to hide her shock. "How do you know?"

Janice winked. "I just know, that's all."

Trudy turned to Charlie and gave him a meaningful look. He was the one who had a relationship with Janice. Like an uncle, the younger woman had said. He needed to step in.

By the grace of God, he got the message. Charlie leaned toward Janice. "Did somebody tell you?" he asked.

She emptied her champagne flute and waved it in the air. "Nobody told me. Figured it out for myself."

Charlie's face beamed at her like she was a niece who'd just pleased him no end. "You're doing lots better'n me. I'm still working on it."

Trudy sat back and watched Charlie at his best.

Janice put her empty flute down on the coffee table. "You don't sleep with Rodney." She looked around and called out. "Where's the champagne? I need some champagne."

Charlie handed her his glass. "Here, have mine. Haven't touched it." He smiled like the uncle she wanted him to be. "We don't want anyone to come in and find us here, do we?"

Janice took the flute. "Thank you, Uncle Charlie."

"So Rodney told you?" he asked.

"Already said, figured it out for myself." She reclined against the abundant cushions and pouted. "Rodney never tells me anything.

Thinks I'm dumb. Maybe I didn't go to college like he did, but I can add up two and two."

"So what did you add up?" Charlie said.

Janice recollected her champagne and took a big swig. "Old Rodney talks in his sleep. Did you know that?"

Charlie gave her a solemn shake of the head and kept quiet. Trudy tried to shrink into the background as far as she could.

"Well, he does, and the night Suzie died, he kept saying, 'It was an accident. Didn't mean to do it.' Said it just plain as day, even though he was asleep."

Trudy couldn't help herself. She had to ask, "Who didn't mean to do it?"

Janice studied her like she'd just seen Trudy for the first time. "Well, Rodney, of course. Who else? Somehow he killed Suzie, but he didn't mean to do it." Janice laughed like a witch in a Grade-B movie. "Imagine that. Old Rodney got rid of his first wife, and I won't have to worry about *her* no more."

Alice was about to turn in when her phone rang. It was Charlie, and his voice sounded so excited, it was obvious the call was important. "We're on our way. Get everybody together. Boy, have we got news."

She phoned all the Silver Foxes, including Anne-Marie who was now back at Evergreen. Alice wondered whether Anne-Marie had been able to control herself at the Open House. The petite woman knew a lot about what the Silver Foxes were doing. Would she have told any of the Cunninghams? By the time Trudy and Charlie hustled through Alice's door, everyone was assembled. Most were in PJs and robes. Anne-Marie was still wearing her party dress, though her makeup, like her whole demeanor, looked tired.

Alice had held places for Trudy and Charlie on the couch, and the two sat side-by-side telling the story, a bit from one, a bit from the other. When Charlie relayed Janice's last line about figuring out that Rodney killed Suzie, Anne-Marie threw her hands over her ears and exclaimed, "No!" At the same time, Fred pumped a fist in the air and said, "Yes!"

"What else did Janice say?" George asked.

"That was it," Trudy responded. "Charlie did a great job of getting her to talk, but she seemed to realize she'd gone too far and bolted out of the room."

"We started for Evergreen right after," Charlie added.

"Nothing about Alejandro?" Alice asked. "Forcing him off the road?"

"Not a word," Charlie said, trying to scratch under his soft boot-cast. "Didn't even get a chance to ask."

Fred was about to speak, but Willard held up his hand for silence and said, "What happens next?"

Fred gave Willard a dirty look. "We nail the sucker."

Trudy frowned and shook her head. "Janice's tale isn't proof. Just another possible clue. Besides, what about Alejandro?"

Alice nodded. "Maybe Bethanne and friends have something on that. We need to meet with them, share what we know and find out what they've discovered."

George's voice sounded like he'd been holding in a bushel of exasperation. "Then we go to the Sheriff."

Over in the corner, Anne-Marie looked inconsolable.

Fred and Willard walked back to their apartments through silent corridors. Fred took Willard by the elbow. "What the hell's the matter with everyone? Clear as day from the start." He shook Willard's arm and practically bellowed, "Rodney did it."

Willard took his arm back and gestured for quiet. "Keep it down. Folks are trying to sleep."

Fred stopped in his tracks. "No! You shut the hell up. I'm tired of you putting me down. Telling me to turn up my hearing aid. Ke me from saying what I want to say."

Now it was Willard's turn to take Fred by the elbow. "Come on, ol' buddy. We're tired. Let's get to bed."

"And that's another thing. Stop jerking me around, you tub of..."

Willard let go and backed off, hands in the air.

"Yeah, that's right," Fred growled. "Back off and stay off."

Totally dumbfounded, Willard watched Fred stomp down the hall. It was the first real fight they'd ever had.

Alice was able to reserve the Game Room on short notice, so the Silver Foxes and Bethanne's friends met the next day after Gifts-n-Such closed. She was relieved to be spared the catering because Trudy promised Christmas cookies from her own kitchen, and Mae pledged homemade fruitcake.

Now, as Alice watched everyone helping themselves to coffee or tea and sweets, she wondered if all this Christmas sugar was too much of a good thing. Everyone seemed over-energized, bubbling over with chatter. Besides, several of the Foxes were pre-diabetic, and they appeared to have no intention of keeping that in mind.

Everyone took their seats. Alice noticed Fred and Willard

sitting on opposite sides of the group. That had never happened before. Those two buddies always sat together. What was going on?

Bethanne looked around the assembled teams and smiled. "Do you mind if we go first?"

Alice thought Fred looked like he was exploding with the need to say something right away, but he grudgingly nodded his agreement to listen.

Bethanne glanced at Mae, and the two women seemed to have a moment of communion, silent messages passing back and forth. Mae took a deep breath, almost a shudder, and told what she'd learned from Penelope.

"Guess that leaves Greg Pendergast out for sure," Eden said, looking disgruntled at having to make this admission. "He hasn't been on the up-and-up, but he didn't kill Miz Suzie." She turned her head to look at Jimmy Lee, who nodded and smiled down at her.

Meanwhile, Fred was half-rising from his seat. "What Penelope said doesn't mean a damn thing. Rodney could've smothered Suzie after his daughter ran away."

"Time enough to speculate later," Alice said. "Let Charlie and Trudy tell the others what they learned last night. Then we'll all be on the same page."

Fred lowered his bum with ill grace, but at least he kept still. Across the group, Alice saw Willard give Fred a nod of approval.

When Charlie and Trudy had finished telling what Janice had said, George spoke up. "The two stories dovetail some, but not exactly. Penelope says she caused her mother to have a heart attack. Janice thinks Rodney killed Suzie after Penelope left. Both could be true. First the heart attack, then murder."

"Then who killed Alejandro?" Alice asked.

"Rodney," said Fred. "Didn't want his baby girl to get the blame for something he did."

Anne-Marie raised her eyes to heaven like she needed something she might not get.

Charlie countered. "Maybe Rodney was talking about Penelope doing something when he said, 'Accident. Didn't mean to do it.' The man was talking in his sleep, not trying to put somebody off the scent."

Trudy shook her head. "Let's face it. Penelope could have done both. If she killed her mother by getting her too upset or even smothering her, and then noticed Alejandro in the hallway..."

Fred interrupted. "Have you noticed how wimpy she is now? Penelope isn't the feisty girl she was in college. No way she's got the guts to pull it off."

Mae looked distressed at having to speak. "She's tiny, and she's sweet as can be most of the time. But she started slanting the truth about as soon as she could talk. And I saw her throw a tantrum more than once. Not just when she was a child, but also when she was a teenager." Mae's breath huffed out like she'd been holding in all kinds of things. "And when she was like that, she'd break things. Her mother's china figurines, her sister's dolls."

"That's when she was a kid," Fred said. "What's she done lately?"

It looked to Alice like Anne-Marie just couldn't take it anymore. Her voice, normally gentle, exploded with emotion. "I can't imagine Penelope could be that spiteful. I've been with her many times as a child and an adult and never seen that side of her."

Nodding at Anne-Marie's defense of Penelope, Willard licked his forefinger and used it to pick up the rest of his fruitcake crumbs.

He put the crumb-encrusted finger in his mouth and grinned at Fred. The retired dentist grinned back like Willard had scored the winning point.

Watching the assembly's failure to come together, Alice was in despair. Would they never get to the bottom of what happened?

27

ON THE WAY HOME AFTER THE MEETING, Eden asked Jimmy Lee to pull over at the Quik Treet. He couldn't believe it. "You still hungry after all them sweets?"

"No, but I need to talk. Let's go round to the back."

Jimmy Lee parked in front of a trio of blue spruce, and Eden thought they only needed some snow to look Christmasy this time of year. He pivoted his body toward her. "What's on your mind? Something to do with what we talked about this evening?"

Her smile was wistful. "Think I had a come-to-Jesus moment."

"Yeah?" he asked, careful to keep his voice neutral.

"Yeah," she said. "I was ready to ruin Greg Pendergast's life and his wife's too. Just because I took a disliking to him."

"Over what you thought was him horning in on EverTeen duties?"

"I see now I wanted to get back at him, because I thought he was out-of-line." She paused and hung her head. "I misjudged him. I was prejudiced."

Jimmy Lee reached over and touched her shoulder. "Well, he was where he wasn't supposed to be and doing what he wasn't supposed to be doing. You wasn't wrong about that."

Eden gaze turned up and out toward the blue spruce. "But I was quick to judge. Never occurred to me that Miz Suzie might've asked him to spend time with her. And for sure I never thought she might be doing something nice for him. I misjudged her too. She was one of the kindest people I ever met, and I had no thought except to get Greg Pendergast and get him good."

Jimmy Lee could see her jaw clenching and unclenching. He was ready to say something else, when she continued. "What does that say about me? What kind of person am I to judge others so quick?"

He reached a finger to turn her head toward his, so they could look each other in the eye. "A good person who sometimes gets ahead of herself. Just like we all do. Think about First Corinthians. 'No temptation has overtaken you except what is common to mankind.' But the other side of the coin is that you're brave to act when you see wrong's been done."

"But I went too far."

"Yes, you did," he said and saw her eyes open wide with his agreement. He carried on, so she would know he saw more than he'd said. "If you think about it, I expect you've learned something."

Her voice sounded sad and contrite. "Look before you leap." She shook her head. "Wonder if I'll ever learn that? I must be the most hard-headed girl on the planet."

He smiled. "You made a good start. You see what you done and you're sorry for it. The Lord sees that."

She nodded, and he continued, "Nothing left to do but pray." He held both hands out to her, and she placed hers in his. Then

Jimmy Lee Schuman prayed the most perfect prayer he'd ever prayed in his life, asking the Lord to help Eden be her best self.

When he was done, they both could sense the peace filling her heart. It felt like she'd turned a corner in her life.

Alice watched Fred and Willard leave the meeting side by side like nothing had ever happened between them. Yet something had caused them to sit apart, and another something had brought them together. She shook her head. Two grown men acting like children?

It was a welcome relief from the meeting's tension when George came up and offered to help carry the leftovers back to her place. After they put everything in her fridge, she suggested a glass of wine. "I know I need one after that, and I'll bet you do too."

He reached for the bottle. "Here, let me open that while you get the glasses."

They sat on either end of her brown tweed couch, half-turned toward each other. "Cheers," he said.

"Not so sure what we can cheer about," she said, "but it's good to feel like we're near the end."

He touched his glass to hers. "Let's not talk about that now. I'm just royally sick of the whole thing." Chow-Fan came out from under the couch and sniffed at his striped socks. George put down a hand for her to sniff as well. She bowed her head and deigned to let him rub around her ears, turning her head this way and that, no doubt making sure he touched all the right spots.

George looked around Alice's apartment. "It's so cozy here. I noticed that the first time when I saw your wall of books. I've got a lot of books too, but my place is just a bachelor's pad."

Alice didn't know what to say. She'd never thought of herself as much of a decorator, just putting things where they seemed to belong and getting on with life. She touched a hand to her new bob.

"And I like your new hairdo," he said. "Becomes you."

"Thanks," she contrived to say, still feeling speechless. She desperately needed to change the subject. "I don't know about you, but I think we've got to wind up this search for how Suzie died. What more can we learn?"

George sighed and took a sip of his wine. "I agree, but everybody wanted to let Charlie have one more chance with Janice and Mae one more try with Penelope. See if they can find any connection with Alejandro's death. Regardless of what they do or don't learn, I'll go to Price with what we know." He paused. "When that day comes, I'd like you to go with me."

Alice started to shrug, but he continued. "You're smart and articulate. You'll catch any mistakes I make or things I leave out."

She couldn't recall when she'd ever felt so flustered. Not even her first day of teaching after she got her Ph.D. What was the matter with her? She glanced at her watch. "Gosh. Nearly dinner time. We'd better go."

George sighed again. "I'll walk you over."

Charlie sat through Evergreen's weekly Sunday brunch, eager to get on with one final effort with Janice Cunningham. Then he drove himself to the municipal park track. First time driving, but he only needed his right foot for that, and he was doing okay. Once there, he got out his cane and walked over to take a seat on a bench. Across the field, he could see Janice running in her red track suit, but not with her usual gusto. It was like she was deep in thought, and running was helping her think. But the thoughts weren't happy.

When she got closer, he called out to her and waved. "Looking good."

She glanced in his direction, stopped and then sauntered toward him. It felt to Charlie like she wasn't sure if she should come or not. He waved again and said, "Good to see you. How you doing?"

Janice sat down beside him and hung her head so he couldn't see her face. "Lord, I think I'm still hung over. I had way too much to drink at the Open House. Did I make a fool of myself? What did I say?"

Charlie patted her shoulder. "You didn't make a fool of yourself. It was a Christmas party, for goodness sake. I think all of us had a little too much to drink." He crossed the fingers of his other hand behind his back for telling a fib to make her feel better.

She raised her head to look at him, and he almost choked. Her tumbled hair had hidden the mark of a bruise on her cheek. Janice saw him looking and tried to pull her hair back over the bruise.

"What happened? Looks like somebody smacked you."

Janice touched the bruised cheek. "Rodney slapped me. He was mad at me after the party. Wanted to know what I was doing with you and Trudy in the family room." She tried to smile, but it wasn't working very well. "I like your lady-friend, by the way. She suits you."

Charlie nodded, and Janice rushed on. "But I didn't tell him a thing. Said I was just showing you all around and how much you liked the house."

"So he hit you just for that?"

"No, that seemed to satisfy him. But he was so smug, so sure of himself, and I guess the drink got to me too. Anyway, the words were out of my mouth before I realized it. Said I heard him talking in his sleep, and I knew he killed Suzie. That's when he socked me."

Janice tried to smile again. She put a hand up to her cheek. "Not the first time. Not the worst time. But it hurt pretty good."

"Did he say anything? Or did he just haul off and hit you?"

Janice frowned. "Called me an idiot and claimed he didn't lay a hand on Suzie. Said he tried to save her, but it was too late."

"Did you believe him?"

"I dunno. Maybe."

Charlie put his hand on her forearm, where another bruise had once been. "I'm so sorry. I feel like our visit set him off."

Janice shook her head. "Don't you worry about it. Doesn't take much to set him off." She put her hand over his hand. "I think I'm gonna get me a good lawyer and leave him." She got out a real smile this time. "You truly are like an uncle to me. What do you think?"

Charlie smiled back. "I think I know a good lawyer."

Charlie was thinking of Farnsworth when he said that, but the Silver Fox lawyer was in a quandary just then. George was disconcerted after brunch when Anne-Marie touched his elbow and said, "Can you come to my apartment? I need to talk to you about something." He looked over her shoulder at Alice, trying to send her a message, but it wasn't clear if she understood. Then he nodded and followed Anne-Marie down the hall to her apartment.

If George didn't know it before, he knew it for sure when he entered that apartment. Tom's will had left Anne-Marie more than well-off. This was one of the most spacious apartments at Evergreen, definitely larger than his or any of the others he knew. It had also clearly been decorated by a professional in shades of sage and old rose. Full of antiques, old silver and gilt-framed mirrors, the apartment had that everything-in-the-perfect-place look, not homey and lived-in. Brocade curtains matched a wallpapered alcove featuring an oil portrait of some ancestor with a mahogany table below. On the other wall was a velvet sofa with crystal sconces on either side. This was like a mini-Versailles, with a mini-poodle to match.

"Gigi!" Anne-Marie cried. "Come to Mommy." Gesturing toward the poodle, she said, "I hope you don't mind?" George shook his head. Anne-Marie sat on the sage-green couch and patted a space nearby. George planted himself on the spot, and Gigi jumped up to lie down between them.

Anne-Marie sucked both lips between her teeth, bit down and opened her mouth to speak. "You probably could tell I've been buried in anxiety at our recent meetings. I want to be loyal to the Cunninghams, but you're right, Suzie was a friend too." Her brow furrowed at she watched George. "Where does my duty lie?"

George started to stroke Gigi, but the little dog growled, so he sat back and eyed Anne-Marie. "To the truth. What is the truth about Suzie's death?"

Anne-Marie almost howled. "I don't know. I don't know what's the truth."

George kept his voice low and confidential. "What happened to make you question your duty?"

She kept her head down, looking at her lap and reciting. "I went to the Open House. I was having a good time, just like you told me. Then Brenda came up and said she'd been chewing something over, and I was the only person she felt she could trust." Anne-Marie raised an agonized face. "See? She trusted me, and now I'm going to tell you. So my self-respect goes out the window."

"Sometimes we have to make tough decisions about the lesser

of two evils," he said. "Which is more evil, a murder or betraying trust?"

Anne-Marie's mouth twisted. "Murder, of course, but that doesn't make me feel any better." She exhaled a groan. "All right." She paused, as if to gather breath and courage. "The night Alejandro Garcia died, Penelope called Brenda in a panic. Asked if her sister knew where their father was. Brenda said no, and Penelope hung up. Brenda said she'd been troubled ever since, because she didn't know what to make of it."

She turned to George. "I don't know either. What do you think?"

He smiled, trying to make his suggestion easier for her. "I think you should come with us to the Sheriff."

Anne-Marie turned her whole body away, and Gigi shifted to stay next to her mistress. "I couldn't," she said. "I won't."

George felt like he had all his feelings bottled up inside, trying to get out. "At least let me tell the Sheriff. I'll say I heard this, but I won't reveal the source."

She turned back. "Okay, but don't ask me to say anything to anybody, ever, because I won't betray my friends."

George took in a slow breath to control his frustration, but exhaling didn't dispel the feeling.

28

Mae spent Sunday morning in church like she always did. This time she was praying to the Lord to help her that afternoon. She'd already called Penelope and asked her to meet for one more talk. Penelope had been reluctant, spoke at length about it being the Christmas season, a thousand things to do at her shop and family time too. Mae had prevailed in the end, offering to come to Penelope's boutique in Rodney's shopping center. Bethanne was minding Gifts-n-Such, so Mae could do as they'd agreed.

Now she was standing with Penelope in that little boutique, surrounded by poinsettias, wreaths and boughs of holly, all of them artful but artificial. Last-minute shoppers were thronging the mall, but Penelope had put up a "Back in 15 minutes" sign when Mae walked in. Mae had purposely suggested they meet there, so Penelope would be on her own turf and hopefully more comfortable.

"I don't have much time," Penelope said from across the counter. "Don't want to lose any sales this close to Christmas."

"Don't worry, I won't be long," Mae said and looked around for a place to sit. When there wasn't one to be had, she leaned her wide hip against the counter and tried to be as relaxed as possible. "Been thinking about what you said last time we were together, and that set me to wondering. Did you tell your Daddy about seeing that flower man out in the hospital hallway?"

Penelope regarded at her with squinted eyes, like she was trying to figure out what Mae was getting at and what would be the best answer. "How does it matter? Momma's dead."

Mae kept her voice soft but firm. "So's that man."

The younger woman crossed her arms. "Well, I didn't kill him."

"Means a lot to hear that." Mae paused. "So did you tell your Daddy about him or not?"

Penelope's green eyes narrowed. "You want to know if Daddy killed him."

Mae didn't answer. She just waited.

Penelope backed off from the counter until she ran into the display case behind. Her face turned such a deep red that Mae was afraid she'd keel over. Penelope put her hands back to steady herself. "I'm not saying." Her voice rose. "Now get the hell out of my shop and never ask to see me again. Because you never, ever will."

All the way out of Penelope's shop, through the mall and across the parking lot, Mae willed herself to keep her pain inside. But once in her car, she bowed her head on the steering and let it all out. Then she wiped her eyes, blew her nose and drove on home to warm up the leftovers from Sunday dinner.

Tuesday afternoon, Alice was contemplating the five people sitting in the waiting area of the Sheriff's Office. Maybe they'd been members of the Silver Foxes or Bethanne's group before, but now they were all bound together as friends on a common quest.

The full eleven friends had met previously to exchange the results of Mae's talk with Penelope and Charlie's with Janice.

Everyone had agreed there was no way they could go any further. Fred had put up objections because he wanted to nail Rodney, but even he had to acquiesce in the end. So the five — George, Alice, Bethanne, Mae and Charlie — were delegated to tell Sheriff Price everything the two groups had discovered.

The waiting area was just a bunch of old wooden chairs in the front hallway. The secretary and deputies occupied desks across a wooden barrier with a gate. Everything looked scuffed and worn, including the door to Jerry Price's office. His secretary had been in there a long time after saying she'd let him know they'd arrived for their appointment.

As they waited, Alice noticed Mae bowing her head, hands clasped, eyes shut, lips moving. When it seemed the large woman had finished her prayer, Alice rested a hand on Mae's wrist and said, "You going to be okay?"

Mae laid her plump hand on top of Alice's thin one. "Yes, I am. I'm terribly downhearted about my bond with Penelope being broken. But I can't stand by and let her and her father get away with murder." She paused. "If there was murder, but that's up to the Sheriff, not me."

Alice started to respond, but the door to the Sheriff's office opened. The secretary beckoned them inside and rushed to bring extra chairs from the hallway. Alice stepped back to see how well Charlie was navigating, but George had a hand near his elbow, so she needn't have worried.

Jerry Price sat tilting his desk chair back on its spring, a cigar in one hand and a phone in the other. He put down the phone and gave George a slight smirk. "Didn't know you were going to bring in reinforcements when you said you wanted to talk."

Alice watched George settle with ease into his chair and

admired his poise. He was in his element, and she'd never seen him like that until now. He wore a navy suit and striped tie, looking very professional and speaking to the sheriff with confidence. "I promised to tell you if I learned anything about those deaths, and now I'm here to do that." He gestured with an arm to his companions. "I brought these folks, because each one has a piece of the puzzle." He smiled. "I have one too."

Price sat up in his chair. "You bringing in evidence, conjecture or hearsay?"

George nodded. "A little of each. Not enough for a trial, but certainly enough to open an investigation."

Price leaned back, but not as far as his chair had tilted before. "I'm listening." He drew on his cigar and blew out a smoke ring. Alice wondered how he was feeling. On his guard because he'd let this go and now ready to be defensive?

George put his hands lightly on his knees. "We believe we can establish a connection between the deaths of Susan Cunningham and Alejandro Garcia."

The Sheriff frowned and shook his head. "Mrs. Cunningham? We've got that down as natural causes." He paused and seemed to try to regain some authority. "Both deaths are in my jurisdiction because they were outside city limits." He half-suppressed a laugh. "Guess you know that, or you wouldn't be here. So you think her death wasn't due to natural causes?"

"Maybe yes, maybe no," George said. "Let us present what we know." He gestured at Bethanne. "Mrs. Swanson will start."

Bethanne recounted her attempts to get Alejandro to talk and his finally saying he'd seen a woman running away from Suzie Cunningham's room.

Next came Mae. Alice was apprehensive, but she needn't have been. Mae was as calm and self-assured as ever, telling all she'd learned from her conversations with Penelope. Only at the end did she falter, when she had to recount Penelope's parting words. But even then, she kept that natural dignity which seemed her hallmark from birth.

Then it was Charlie's turn. Alice was afraid he'd go on and on, never being able to focus. But George had rehearsed him, and Charlie sat there with both hands atop his duck-headed cane, relating what Janice had said with nary a tangent.

George brought up the rear, with his account of what the homeless man told the Catholic nun about being "pretty sure" it was a woman who ran Alejandro Garcia off the road and over an embankment. He added what he'd heard from a reliable source who wanted to remain anonymous, that Penelope had called her sister in a panic that night, looking for her father.

Alice watched Sheriff Price listen throughout, taking notes now and then, puffing on his cigar and keeping his face totally devoid of any response to what he was hearing. When everyone had had their say, he spoke up. "Let me see if I got this right." He proceeded to count off the points on his fingers. "One, Penelope says she caused her mother to have a heart attack. Two, Rodney tells Penelope to get out and then hits the call button to save his wife. Three, Alejandro sees Penelope hurrying away and tells at least his sister and Bethanne Swanson. Maybe others too, who knows? Four, Alejandro is run off the road and killed, probably by a woman, but again, who knows? Five, Penelope calls her sister that night, all upset and asking for their father. That about it?" He lifted his eyes to heaven. "Oh wait, Rodney talks in his sleep. Forgot that part."

"We know a lot of this is conjecture," Alice said. "And there are other possible explanations. For example, maybe Rodney or Penelope actually smothered Suzie Cunningham. A nurse who came to administer CPR saw him holding a pillow. Suzie was weak, so it could have been easy. Bottom line, we wanted to lay out the facts and possibilities as we see them and let you decide what to do."

When she finished, she saw George looking at her with admiration.

ιe Sheriff turned to George. "He said, she said. Reliable source wants to remain anonymous. Second-hand gossip. Talking, but not walking, in his sleep. Maybe this, maybe that. Not much in the way of facts, is there, Counselor?"

George nodded. "We've reported what we've learned. It's up to you to find out if there's enough here to go to trial."

"Awfully flimsy," Price said. He put his elbows on his desk, his hands, including the cigar, clasped in front of his face. Alice watched the Sheriff sitting there, clearly reviewing what he'd heard and hopefully thinking about what, if anything, he might do. Would he send them on their way? Say they were wasting his time?

Alice studied her friends. All eyes seemed riveted on Price, their lips parted, almost holding their breaths.

Finally he spoke, his attention fully on George. "Okay, Counselor, you've made your case. Now leave it to me and my deputies. Take your buddies and go on home. We'll look into it, see if we find anything concrete." The Sheriff sent a stern gaze around the group. "If I hear so much as a peep that you all are at it again, I'll slap a citation on the lot of you. Got it?"

Alice tried not to smile in triumph. She dared a peek at George. He looked just like she felt. They'd got what they came for.

29

A FEW NIGHTS LATER, ALICE STOOD in the window of her living room with Chow-Fan twining around her ankles. She'd turned the lights out, so she could enjoy the falling snow. Sure seemed like they were going to have a white Christmas. The snow had started that afternoon and was forecast to continue through tomorrow morning. Already the world had turned white, the parking lot lights silhouetting black branches and dark evergreens against the blowing flakes. The scene brought back memories of childhood, coming in from sledding and having hot chocolate.

She sighed. That was before polio cost her so much of that childhood, keeping her in bed or in physical therapy, trying to make those limp muscles work again. She did a slight knee-bend and thanked her lucky stars those painful exercises had succeeded. She was a survivor, able to live a fairly normal life. She just had to deal now with the weakness on her left side from the overused nerve and muscle cells that remained. Maybe she'd never be a ballerina, but she'd done most things she'd wanted, even joining a moderate hiking vacation in Italy when she'd saved up enough to afford it.

She watched a couple making their way from the Independent Living entrance to a car parked as near as possible to the front door.

What a night to have to go out, she thought. But it was the Christmas season, lots of parties, and who'd want to miss a little fun?

As they came under a streetlight, Alice realized she was looking at Anne-Marie and George. She'd lost track of when the Country Club dinner-dance was scheduled, but this must be the night. Under his open black overcoat and white neck scarf, George had on a traditional tux with a black bow tie. None of that silly seasonal plaid or red or green. So like him to be that classic, a gentleman of the old school. She'd never seen him look more handsome.

On his arm, Anne-Marie teetered in those ridiculously high sandals, probably getting her feet soaked. She had on a soft-beige mink jacket that beautifully set off her gold lamé dress. She must have had her hair done that afternoon, because every strand of it was flawlessly in place despite a fairly stiff wind tossing the snow flakes here and there.

Alice touched a hand to her own new hairdo, remembering George saying he liked it. Probably just being polite, but still she found herself wondering what he thought of her. A dreary spinster trying too hard? Certainly not the glamorous Anne-Marie with lots of money to spend on her looks.

By now, George had handed Anne-Marie into the car and got into the driver's seat. They drove off into the falling snow, and Alice turned to make herself a cup of cocoa.

Lewiston did have a white Christmas, and the Silver Foxes gathered around their usual lunch table to celebrate. They each seemed to have on a touch of red, a sweater or a tie for the men, a dress or a scarf for the women. Only Anne-Marie was different, wearing a Kelly-green jersey dress that showed off her bosom to good effect.

Once they'd been served with turkey and all the trimmings, Alice was pleased when Trudy took the initiative. The grandmother held out her hands right and left and said, "Let's remember our absent friend." Their clasped hands encircled the table, as each silently recalled Suzie being there the year before and deeply missed this year.

As a general rule, they never said grace, letting each person follow his or her own path in that regard. But this time, Willard surprised Alice by saying, "We ask your blessing on our sister Susan and on each of us here tonight. It's been a difficult time for all of us, and we hope for peace in the New Year." All around the table, a chorus of "Amen" sounded from baritones, tenors, altos and sopranos.

George complimented Trudy and the decorating committee for how beautifully they'd captured the season. As always, they'd used real greenery and a live tree with ornaments donated or made by Evergreen residents. Trudy pointed out a series of tiny lanterns constructed from wooden matchboxes and painted in bright colors. "Made by the mother of one of our residents during the shortages of World War II," Trudy said. "So fragile and so precious."

Fred seemed compelled to add, "Thank God we didn't have to worry about Charlie on a ladder this time." Charle appeared to take the jab in stride, and Willard just rolled his eyes like "What else did you expect?"

Anne-Marie seized the spotlight with a long discourse on the Country Club dance, ending with the proposal that she reserve a table for all of them next year, so everyone could experience the magical evening. With the word "magical," she gave George a kilowatt smile, and he nodded in her direction. When there were no immediate takers of her invitation, Anne-Marie said they could think about it and let her know.

Throughout all this, Alice kept quiet. Her eyes circled the table. She was disconcerted to see George watching her. What did that look mean? Her thoughts began to roam. What would the New Year bring? Would Sheriff Price follow through? If so, what would come of it? Had all their work been for nothing? She just wanted it to be over.

Bethanne was enjoying Christmas with Mae's family. Big Jim's hearty bass was encouraging everyone to hurry up and open their presents so they could get to the food. Their daughter and grandchild passed around the gifts, and the little girl was soon happily surrounded by torn wrappings and ribbons.

Bethanne had brought presents for everyone. When the time came for her and Mae to exchange gifts, she almost lost it when she discovered they'd selected the same thing for each other, an engraved locket. Even the sentiments were nearly the same, expressing thanks for the life they'd shared and looking forward to the years to come. By the time each had put her locket on, both were wiping away the tears.

"Okay, ladies," Big Jim said. "Christmas is a time for tears of sharing and joy, but right now, my stomach is growling about sharing sugar-cured ham with cornbread and pan gravy." He laughed to show he was only teasing, trying to keep the two friends from getting maudlin. Big Jim gestured toward the table and helped his daughter settle his grandchild into a highchair. Mae and Bethanne hurried into the kitchen to dish up the food.

And what a lot of dishes there were. Mae must have been cooking for days, Bethanne reflected. Not only ham and cornbread but candied yams, green beans, homemade cranberry sauce with ground oranges and nuts, biscuits and apple butter. Never one to cook, let alone cook well, Bethanne helped get the dishes on the table and serve the white wine she'd brought.

As usual, Mae was lavish with baking, offering both mince pie as well as individual fruitcakes that had been aging in bourbon for a month. Bethanne had bought something special to drink with dessert, a festive and sweet champagne.

Afterwards, Bethanne and Mae shooed the other three into the living room while they cleaned up the kitchen. This was their time to be together. Bethanne put a hand to her locket. "I guess you know how much this means to me."

"I guess you know how proud I am to be your friend," Mae responded. "I know you're friends with Eden, and I'm proud of that too. You've both come so far since you first came to town." She paused and put both hands on Bethanne's shoulders. "You never take a drink now, even though you brought the wine. Does it make you feel bad to see us drinking? Or eating that bourbon-soaked cake while you make do with mince pie?"

Bethanne lightly gripped Mae's wrists. "Not at all. I go to AA at least once a week to make sure I stay strong. I like myself better sober. I expect everyone else does too." She grinned. "Come on, let's get this mess cleaned up, so we can enjoy the rest of the day."

Eden and Jimmy Lee spent Christmas morning with their families at the Church of the Holy Light. Pastor Bob Marvin preached like the angels had come down to inspire him. Afterwards, the Schumann and Jones families stood in the social hall and hugged each other all around.

Mrs. Jones stood on tiptoe to embrace Jimmy Lee. "I know you and Eden ain't boyfriend and girlfriend no more," she said. "But

I thank God everyday that you come into her life. Eden always was a good girl, but you helped her mellow out some. She needed that."

Jimmy Lee found himself so tongue-tied, he just nodded. Finally he found the words. "Well if I did, it was God working through me, and I'm thankful for that."

Jimmy Lee's momma was trying to corral the other four kids, and Eden went after her five year-old brother, Chase, who'd spied the Christmas cookies and couldn't wait to grab one. She managed to scoop him up and bring him back to the fold without so much as a hint of vexation in his voice or face.

Pastor Bob came over. "Eden, you've got a way with kids. Ever thought about being a pediatrician? I think you have the knack for it."

She let Chase swing back and forth from their locked hands. "Thank you kindly. Too soon to tell, really. Let me get through med school. Then maybe I'll know enough about medicine and myself to make the right choice."

He patted her on the shoulder. "I'll be praying on that."

30

THE HOLIDAY SEASON CHUGGED ON, heavy snow keeping most Evergreen residents indoors. No point in Charlie going to the track to see if Janice was there, because the track was a foot deep in white stuff. Trudy and Anne-Marie both had bad colds, and Willard and Fred were resigned to not playing golf for a while. Alice loved looking out her window at the snow, but she loved staying in with a good book even more.

As New Year's drew near, snowplows cleared most of the roads and parking lots, so things were looking up as far as getting out and about was concerned. Alice found herself fretting because there still was no word from Sheriff Price about investigating Suzie's and Alejandro's deaths. Then the day before New Year's Eve, Alice's phone rang not long after breakfast.

"Sheriff just called," George said. "Wanted to give us fair warning of a televised press conference at three this afternoon. Should we get everybody together at your place?"

"Definitely," she said and proceeded to phone everyone, including Bethanne, inviting all eleven friends to watch and discuss afterwards.

It was their slow season, so Bethanne and Mae closed up Gifts-n-Such and arrived a few minutes early. High school was in recess for the holidays, and Eden hitched a ride with Jimmy Lee. Trudy and George brought extra chairs from their apartments. Everyone could sit, even if they were pretty crowded. Alice had ordered an urn of coffee from Evergreen's kitchen, and Mae brought a lemon sheet cake big enough and easy enough to serve all.

Ten minutes before the press conference was due to start, George turned on the TV with the sound down. The end of some soap opera was on, but nobody paid any attention, the chitchat all devoted to what Jerry Price was going to say.

At three o'clock sharp, the local announcer interrupted with breaking news, and George turned the sound up. The scene shifted to the City Hall Assembly Room and the Mayor walking up to a microphone-decked podium, followed by the Sheriff and the County Attorney. The Foxes kept shifting in their seats while they waited for the Mayor to finish his political speech about the advantages of county and city working together. Finally, he introduced Jerry Price.

Price looked completely at home. "Good afternoon and thanks for coming on such short notice. We made an arrest this morning, and the Mayor and I agreed that we wanted to have a press conference before rumors start flying. I'm going to read a statement, and then we're both available for questions, along with the County Attorney. I hope you can appreciate that we might not be able to answer every question in a case that's going to court."

He glanced around the crowd of reporters, both print and radio/TV, as if to make sure they understood what he'd just said. Then he read from his prepared statement.

"At eight a.m. today, we arrested Rodney Cunningham..."

"Yes!" Fred interrupted, and Anne-Marie gasped. But all ears and eyes were still on Jerry Price. Alice sat quietly, waiting for the rest of the story to unfold. This was what they'd worked so hard for, but the story wasn't over.

"...for the murder of Alejandro Garcia this past fall. Mr. Cunningham has confessed to the crime and is cooperating fully with authorities. Our investigation over many weeks..."

"Damn liar," Fred said. "Didn't investigate a thing 'til we pushed you."

"Shhhhh," sounded throughout the room, as the Sheriff continued. "... has revealed a number of interconnected facts that we didn't want to make known until we had everything completely in hand." He paused and looked at the reporters again. "One, Rodney Cunningham's wife, Susan, died of a heart attack after an argument with her daughter, Penelope Flynn. Two, Mr. Cunningham wanted to protect his daughter from criticism, so he told her to run away from the hospital room where her mother was dying. Three, as Penelope Flynn was hurrying down the hallway, she was observed by Alejandro Garcia, who told a number of people that he saw an unknown woman running away. Four, both father and daughter came to hear of these allegations, and they were concerned that Penelope would be blamed for her mother's death. Five, Rodney Cunningham took it upon himself to protect his daughter once again by following Mr. Garcia and running him off the road and down an embankment, thus ending his life. Mr. Cunningham confessed to these facts in the early hours of this morning after an intensive interrogation at which his attorney was present."

Hands were already waving from the press, and the Sheriff said, "Okay. I see a lot of questions here. Let me remind you that I probably can't answer all of them, especially about physical evidence, but I'll answer those I can." He nodded at a blond from the local TV station.

She spoke into her hand-held mike. "Our own investigations uncovered that a witness to Garcia's death said that a woman ran him off the road. How does that fit with what you've just said? Did Penelope Flynn kill Garcia, and her father is covering up for her?"

Price smiled like she was some grade school kid who'd got it all wrong. "We also heard that rumor. But it was hearsay. We interviewed that witness the night of Mr. Garcia's death and again the next day. At that time, he said he couldn't be sure if it was a man or a woman driving the other car. It was only later, after the witness had left for parts unknown that we heard this rumor, with no way to check it. We stand with what the witness said at the time of the incident and with Rodney Cunningham's statement."

The blond had a follow-up question. "Did you also bring in Penelope for questioning?"

"Yes, we did, because we heard the same things you did. She admitted to upsetting her mother so badly that Mrs. Cunningham seemed to be having a heart attack. She also confessed that she ran away when her father told her to, seeing Alejandro Garcia in the hall, although she didn't know who he was at that time. Finally, she conceded that she talked to her father about Mr. Garcia, but she firmly denied having anything to do with his death. Mr. Cunningham's confession verified what she said."

A reporter with the *Lewiston Inquirer* was recognized next. "Any evidence that either Penelope or her father actually killed Susan Cunningham? There's been gossip to that effect. Mrs. Cunningham could have been smothered with a pillow, and that contributed to her heart attack."

Price smiled again. "Gossip is gossip. There's no proof of those allegations."

"But it *is* a fact that the family had Susan Cunningham cremated right away," said another reporter. "So any such proof would have been destroyed."

The Sheriff appeared at a loss for words, and the County Attorney stepped in. "Folks, let's not try this case in the Assembly Room. I'm confident the Sheriff has done his job, so we've got the evidence and the right person to take to court. If Rodney Cunningham continues to plead guilty, that'll be a pretty routine session with no necessity for a jury trial."

With that, the County Attorney, Jerry Price and the Mayor left the podium. The reporters shouted after them, "What evidence?" "Tire tracks?" "Paint transfer on Garcia's fender?" But the three men disappeared through the door, and the reporters were left to kibitz.

George turned off the TV, and Alice surveyed the room. Both Mae and Anne-Marie were quietly in tears. Fred looked victorious and disgruntled at the same time. Everyone else looked thoughtful.

Willard turned his gaze to George. "So how will it end up? Who's representing Cunningham?"

George shook his head. "If Rodney sticks to his confession, the court appearance should be cut and dried. His lawyer will just try to make sure he gets his rights and as short a sentence as possible. Play up a father's love for his daughter. Not sure who's representing him. Doubt Farnsworth took the case. Maybe some of those younger guys who started up a firm a few years ago. They might need the income." He shrugged. "Rodney's got lots of money, he may bring in some hotshot from outside. But if he's confessed and wants to stick to it, he probably won't need that kind of talent."

Bethanne said, "Hard to feel satisfied with this, But I guess we can be relieved that someone's being brought to justice for Alejandro's death."

Eden's voice was full of emotion. "Yes, but is it the right someone?"

Jimmy Lee started to speak, but Charlie butted in with a clarification for George. "So you're saying it's unlikely Suzie being murdered will be brought up? No one to pursue the possibility that Rodney or Penelope did it?"

"Price is probably satisfied to be able to put Rodney away for one murder. With a confession to boot. He doesn't need two convictions when there's virtually no evidence for Suzie."

Fred's voice was bitter, and he spoke through clenched teeth. "Not much evidence for killing Garcia either. Nothing at the scene. Nothing at the body shops. Suzie cremated. Pillowcase washed long ago. Only witness dead. The bastard."

Trudy had brought her handwork, the start of a crocheted vest. "Not necessarily. You have to give Rodney credit for trying to save his daughter."

"Bastard," Fred repeated. "Hundred bucks says he'll get away with it."

Alice nodded at Jimmy Lee. "You were going to say something?"

Jimmy Lee smiled his thanks at Alice but directed his gaze at Eden. "Sometimes you gotta be satisfied with what you get, even if it's not what you want."

31

ALICE WOKE THE NEXT MORNING feeling as dissatisfied as she had all through the press conference and the discussion that followed. They'd done all they could, not just the Silver Foxes, but Bethanne and her group too. What more could they have done? Alice found herself without answers.

She went to the Evergreen Cafe for coffee at midmorning, hoping George would show up as he'd been doing most days for a long while. But he didn't come, and neither did any of the other Silver Foxes, even though one or more had dropped by from time to time. Was everyone feeling as despondent as she was?

The more she thought about it, the more she thought George and Fred had got it right. Rodney would go to court, his confession would be entered, and it would all be over, probably in a matter of hours. None of the other possibilities would be allowed to be introduced, and Rodney would get what he wanted. He'd save his darling Penelope one more time. Besides, maybe he *had* killed Alejandro, so he should be punished. The only question would be how long a sentence he'd get. Meanwhile, Penelope would be free to raise her children, despite any guilt she might feel. Maybe there was a kind of justice to that, an older man accepting the blame, so the youngest generation wouldn't suffer a breakup of the family.

Over in Bethanne's apartment above Gifts-n-Such, she and Mae were having much the same conversation. The shop was closed for the long New Year's weekend, and Bethanne had invited Mae to join her for tea and talk.

"You were crying yesterday," Bethanne said.

Mae nodded. "I was thinking about how that baby girl's seeds were sown before she could walk. The youngest child and spoiled to death. Daddy's little princess. Always got what she wanted. Everybody ready to fix whatever mess she got herself into. Looks like the rest of her life will be the same."

"Guess we'll probably never know what really happened."

"Guess not." Mae grimaced. "But Mr. Rodney is paying the price for how that girl was raised."

"Penelope will pay a price too. As long as she lives, whenever she passes, folks will wonder if she killed her mother. That will take a toll." Bethanne sighed and sipped her tea. "Jimmy Lee's right. No point still digging in the muck. New Year tomorrow. Let's look to the future."

Mae raised her cup. "Happy New Year."

Bethanne clicked hers with Mae's. "Happy New Year, old friend."

When Eden came through the door of the Evergreen Cafe, Alice was still sitting there, feeling a little better now she'd thought through the unconventional justice of Rodney confessing.

"I'm sorry to bother you, Miz Dundee," the girl said, "but Miz Trudy told me you often come here for coffee. I just finished over at

Skilled Nursing, and I thought I'd take a chance. Do you mind if I sit down?"

Alice was caught off-guard but endeavored not to show it. "Not at all," she said, gesturing to a chair. "Can I offer you something? Hot drink? Pastry?"

Eden shook her head. "I don't want to trouble you any more'n I have to." The teenager squirmed in her chair like she was trying to find the right words.

Meanwhile, Alice was striving to figure out what on earth had brought her here. They hardly knew each other, except for the joint group meetings.

"Miz Dundee..." Eden started, then changed course. "Should I call you Dr. Dundee?"

Alice smiled. "I'm long retired. Don't use that title anymore. Why don't you call me Alice?"

Eden was squirming again. "I don't think I'd be comfortable with that." She paused, her face scrunched with worry. "See, I want to ask you a favor, and I don't want to take anything for granted."

"What kind of favor?" Then Alice remembered Eden looking at her when she'd introduced herself as a retired professor. Alice smiled. "Something to do with math?"

Eden's face broke into an incredulous grin, and she let her request all out in a rush. "How'd you know? Yes, please. I want to ask you to help me with calculus. I'm up for a pre-med scholarship, and I need to ace the final exam." She sucked in a big breath.

Alice leaned across the table. "Eden, you just made my day. Nothing I like more than helping bright young people conquer math. When would you like to start?"

Eden leaned forward, her face so earnest Alice felt her eyes sting with emotion. "Would it be too much to start right after New Year's?" the girl said. "My exam is on the eighth."

The Silver Foxes worked hard to put their emotional reactions to Sheriff Price's announcement behind them. Time to get ready for Evergreen's annual New Year's Eve dinner dance. For the men, it was a matter of shower and shave, put on suit and tie. For the women, a lot more was involved.

Still buoyed up by the opportunity to help a bright teenager with math, Alice was blow-drying her hair. She was trying to recreate the new style, but without much success. Alice got it smooth enough, but the shape wasn't as bouffant as Tammy had done it. She stood back from the mirror. What the heck. Good enough.

Anne-Marie spent the afternoon pampering herself. She felt like she needed it after the last few weeks. She had a long soak in bubblebath with a moisturizing face masque, touched up her manicure and pedicure, then unwrapped the protective netting she'd had on her hair. It still looked nearly as good as when Tammy had done it yesterday morning. Anne-Marie gazed at her undergarments spread out on the bed, remembering the Country Club dance. Time to put them on again. Would George remain as courtly and correct as he'd been at the Club? It'd been a pleasant enough evening but not really what she'd hoped for. She picked up the Spanx and sighed. Oh well, time for another try.

Trudy stood in front of the mirror on her closet door and viewed her reflection. Her hair in curlers, her feet in fluffy slippers and her blue silk dress getting the once-over. Was this dress too young for her? Should she wear something else? What? Everyone had already seen her other holiday dress at Christmas. She twisted to look at the back. Wasn't much better from that view. She felt like a teenager going to the prom and worrying she had the wrong clothes. "Get over it," she said to the reflection in the mirror. "You're a grown-up now."

Eden and Jimmy Lee would each be celebrating New Year's Eve with their families. But that afternoon, they were having hot chocolate at the Quik Treet before heading on home.

"You feeling okay?" Jimmy Lee asked. "This fall and winter been kinda rough on you."

Eden smiled, sort of a sad, rueful smile. "Yeah, I'm okay. Lot of that stress was my own doing. I see that now." Her smile became a little happier, and she put her hand on his arm. "I'm letting go of all that and looking forward to next year."

His voice turned doleful. "At the University. Far from here, and you're gonna be super-busy."

Now her smile was full and warm. "But never so busy or so far that I don't feel you near. We'll always be part of each other."

32

The Silver Foxes entered the Evergreen dining room together and stood in awe. Alice felt beyond impressed. Also a little guilty. Despite all the recent demands on Trudy's time, she and her decorating committee had outdone themselves. Fairy lights twinkled from the ceiling, where a silver ball revolved and sent particles of light dancing throughout the room. Each table had silver candles and paperwhite narcissus, as well as silver New Year's hats for every chair.

Alice put her arm around Trudy's shoulders. "It's truly magical. Where did you get those flowers? They're just splendid."

Trudy's voice wavered, like the answer was too much for her. "Blossoms Aplenty. In memory of Alejandro."

Charlie still had his orthopedic boot and cane, but he put his arm around Trudy's waist from the other side. "You are one special woman. They surely broke the mold once God got done making you."

"No doubt of that," George said and led them to their round table. Typical of him, Alice thought, guiding us away so we stop blocking the door. He looked more than usually dapper this evening, his charcoal-gray suit set off by a burgundy tie, both pulled together by a white shirt with thin, faint stripes in those colors.

When they were seated, Alice noticed the one chair missing

and last year's alternation of man-woman around the table now changed forever. Somehow, she'd missed that change at Christmas, even though they'd joined hands to remember Suzie. Tonight, George sat between Anne-Marie and Alice, while Charlie and Trudy were on Alice's other side. That left Anne-Marie with two men on her right, but it couldn't be helped. At least Willard was next to her, with Fred next to Trudy.

"Come on," said Willard, reaching for a silver bowler. "Time to put our party hats on." Anne-Marie balked, saying she didn't want to mess up her hair, but George handed her a tiara, and she joined the rest of the Silver Foxes in New Year's finery.

The server arrived with champagne flutes for everyone and the gentle reminder that this first glass was a gift from Evergreen with a no-host wine bar available afterwards. The courses soon arrived, a salad of marinated winter vegetables, a choice of roast beef or salmon with rice pilaf and Brussels sprouts, followed by the option of yogurt parfait or German chocolate cake. Throughout the meal, it seemed to Alice like everyone was making a good-faith effort to be festive, but it fell just a little flat.

Then the trio hired for the occasion began to play golden oldies, and everyone's spirits lifted with *Sweet Caroline*. Charlie whispered something to Trudy, and she whispered back, shaking her head. He smiled at the group. "I'm asking Trudy to dance, and she thinks I'm not up to it. But I'd sure like to try. What do you think?"

George held out a hand and helped him up. "Tell you what, Charlie. If it's no-go, give me a high sign, and I'll help you off the floor and back here." He turned to Trudy. "How does that sound?"

Her look was dubious, but she rose and took Charlie's arm. George asked Anne-Marie to dance, and Willard followed suit with

Alice. To her wonderment, the big man was light on his feet and moved with grace. Alice kept her eyes on Charlie and Trudy, but they seemed to be doing okay. Once on the dance floor, they stood there and just bobbed in time to the music, but Charlie looked pleased as Punch, even if Trudy seemed apprehensive.

Meanwhile, Fred was left to himself. Alice watched him go over to a nearby table of women without partners and promise to dance with each of them before the evening was over. He extended his hand to the first one with a flourish.

When the initial song was over, Alice pleaded weakness in her left leg and sat down. She took a long look at Fred and at herself. She had to admit that maybe Fred's facade was irascible, but deep down, he was kind and thoughtful.

For the second song, George stayed with Anne-Marie, but Fred cut in on Charlie, handing him his cane, so he could limp back to the table.

"Guess I'm still not as strong as I want to be," he said. "Need to sit this one out anyway."

"Didn't know Fred was such a good dancer," Willard said with a grin. "Guess he's got his hearing aid turned up so he can hear the beat."

Alice watched George and Anne-Marie dance to *Unchained Melody*. They made a good couple, and they moved together like they'd been doing it for years.

Then it was time for the partners to switch again. George brought Anne-Marie back to the table, where Willard promptly claimed her. Fred asked Alice to dance, but she again pleaded her weak leg, while George led Trudy onto the floor. That left Charlie and Alice to commiserate about wonky legs and Fred to invite another of the unaccompanied ladies to dance.

Afterwards, he headed for the bar and brought back champagne for all the Foxes. They sat out a few tunes with fizz tickling their noses and talk of who was going where for vacation in the coming year. Most were staying in the States, but Alice had been saving for a University tour of Greece.

"Aren't you brave to go alone?" Anne-Marie said. "I've always been so used to traveling with Tom." She shrugged. "Guess I'll have to book one of those tours or find someone else to travel with." She turned to George with a bright smile, but he appeared engrossed in the play of sparkling lights on his champagne.

Coffee came, and they all seemed comfortable just to sit together and watch the others dance. Then George stood and held out his hand to Alice. She started to demur again, but Trudy pushed her up and said, "Go on, you've rested your leg enough. Besides, that's *Chances Are*. She grinned. "You can manage a slow dance."

Alice tried to acquiesce with good grace, but she felt awkward. George led her out on the floor, held her lightly in his arms and said, "I've never seen you look more lovely. I like the way you dress. You have your own style. But tonight, you look ....."

She didn't know what to say, so she just came out with. "Kind of you."

"Not kind," he said. "True."

To her surprise, they danced well together. She'd never thought of herself as much of a dancer, but George led her around the floor as if she'd been studying at Arthur Murray since childhood. She wondered if he'd taken dancing lessons at some point in life.

He kept her on the floor when the song ended, just like he had with Anne-Marie. She supposed that must be his usual practice, two dances, then switch partners. But when a third tune started, he ushered her to the wine bar, handed her a glass of champagne and said, "Are you tired of the crowd? Let's go to the Game Room where we can have some peace and quiet."

Alice glanced at their table where everyone was laughing about something and then followed George out of the dining room and down the hall. The Game Room was set up as usual with card tables and chairs, but George led her to the couch, and they sat down at either end.

His gaze drifted around the room. "Lot of happy hours here as partners."

"Yes," she said, "we play bridge well together."

"I'm thinking about another kind of partnership," he said. "I think we should get married."

Alice gasped. "What about Anne-Marie?"

"What about her?"

"You took her to the Country Club dance."

"Don't you feel sorry for her?" he said. "I do. So lost without Tom. Kids and grandkids on the other side of the country. I thought the least I could do was be her escort for one night."

Alice sat there with her mouth open, unable to say a word.

George turned to face her, his arm extending along the back of the couch. "I've loved you for a long time, maybe ever since I looked at your books and realized how much we have in common."

She started to laugh, her nerves getting the best of her, but he put fingertips over her mouth and continued. "The only things I can think of to say are clichés. Two sides of the same coin. Yin and yang. Complete together, incomplete apart. Dammit. Just say you'll marry me, so we can be together for whatever life is left to us."

He took his fingers from her lips, but she still had no words.

She just sat there, wide-eyed, nodding again and again. Then his mouth was on her mouth, and his body was next to hers, and she couldn't remember when things had ever felt this perfect.

After a time, he led her back to the dance floor, and they swayed together as if they could never be separated. On and on, one song after another.

All Silver Fox eyes were on them as the five remaining friends sat this one out.

Trudy and Charlie were still side by side, his hand on the back of her chair. "Don't they make a handsome couple?" she asked.

So do we, he thought and wondered if he could work up the courage to propose by Easter.

Willard threw his giant arm across Fred's diminutive shoulders. "Come on, old friend, let's go get drunk."

Anne-Marie tore her eyes from George and Alice. "Sounds like a good idea to me. Want to go out to the Country Club where they have a real bar? Doesn't look like anybody's going to miss us."

Fred grinned. "Damn straight, sister."

QUESTIONS FOR DISCUSSION

1. This is the final book in my trilogy of West Virginia mysteries. If you were to write the next book, what would be the story? What would happen to each of the Lewiston characters — Eden, Jimmy Lee, Bethanne, Mae, Alice, George, Trudy, Charlie, Anne-Marie, Willard and Fred? What about Rodney, Brenda, Penelope and Janice?

2. What were your first and final impressions of each of the characters (listed above) in this book?

3. Do you think Eden and Jimmy Lee will get back together as more than friends? Why or why not?

4. Did Fred's swearing bother you? Did it seem realistic? What about his tendency to go off half-cocked?

5. Rodney talked his daughters into letting him buy most of the land surrounding the Great Oaks mansion. He may have been cheating them, because the income from his proposed property development might have been more lucrative for his two girls if they had retained title to the land. Did you consider that as you were reading those scenes? If you were Brenda or Penelope, would you sue?

6. What did you think of Anne-Marie's immoderate support for the entire Cunningham family? Did it make you suspicious? In what way?

7. Did George's proposal come as a surprise to you? Why or why not? Will Alice and George be a good match?

8. Will Trudy and Charlie get married? Why do you think that?

9. What will happen to Kathy Pendergast now? Do you think Trudy will be able to persuade someone at church to pay her monthly fee in Memory Care?

10. What do you think really happened? Was Suzie killed? If so, who did it? Who forced Alejandro off the road? Was it believable that Rodney would take the rap in order to get Penelope out of her ultimate scrape and to ensure his grandchildren wouldn't suffer a family breakup? Why?

11. Why do you think Sheriff Price seemed so eager to put this case to rest without further investigation? What additional evidence could he have investigated?

12. Evergreen is a Continuous Care Retirement Community, where residents pay a significant entrance fee and hefty monthly fees in order to be guaranteed lifetime care, including Independent Living, Assisted Living, Skilled Nursing and Memory Care. There's no price increase except for a small yearly percentage tied to inflation. Have you ever considered such a facility for yourself or another family member? Is a CCRC attractive to you? Why or why not?